Artful Deceit

Lily Larkin Mysteries
Book 6

Hannah Ellis

Published by Hannah Ellis
www.authorhannahellis.com
Postfach 900309, 81503 München
Germany

Cover design by dmeacham design

Artful Deceit

Chapter One

In the middle of August, summer on the Isles of Scilly came to a screeching halt. For Lily, the disappearance of warm, sunny days was disheartening in more ways than one. First, there was a noticeable drop in the number of customers at the ice cream shop.

It also meant her romantic picnic with Flynn was postponed.

They'd had other dates – dinners, and evenings in the pub – but nothing that matched the idea of sitting on a secluded beach to watch the sunset together.

After a week of waiting for the weather to improve, Flynn arrived at the ice cream shop with his backpack on his shoulder and a picnic blanket slung over his arm.

"Really?" Lily asked, glancing outside. "You think it's picnic weather?"

"It didn't rain at all today," he said, catching her lips in the briefest kiss.

"It's overcast and chilly," she said. "And the sand will be damp."

"Now you're just making excuses." He glanced around the shop. "Did you have any customers today?"

"A few. Not many."

"Was Jessica here?"

"No. I told her to take the day off." She plucked idly at the fluff on his picnic blanket. "I honestly don't think it's picnic weather."

"Maybe not an outdoor picnic." His lips twitched into a smile. "I thought we could have an indoor one for now."

"That sounds better than sitting on a damp beach."

He kissed her again. "I'm going upstairs to set this up."

"I'll tidy up. I shouldn't be long."

Half an hour later, she went upstairs to find Flynn had moved the furniture in the living room and set up his picnic blanket in the middle of the room. A plate of sandwiches sat beside a bowl of salad and a quiche.

"Thank you," she said, accepting a beer from Flynn as he strolled out of the kitchen.

"The weather will probably pick up again soon," he said, tilting his head. "We'll have that sunset picnic at some point. I promise."

She nodded and took a seat at the edge of the blanket.

"What's wrong?" he asked, sitting beside her and setting a hand on her knee.

"The weather is bothering me," she said grumpily.

"I know you grew up on the continent, but I thought you'd lived in the UK long enough to be used to it."

"I am. It's not just the bad weather though. It's what it signals. The summer is ending, and everything is changing. I don't know if I'm going to like winter here."

He took a long swig of his beer. "You'll be okay."

"I know." She tried not to think about the thing that really bothered her – Flynn's imminent departure to London in two weeks. "Everything will be all right. The weather is just depressing me." With a sigh, she switched her attention to the food. "This looks great."

Flynn filled her in on his day as they ate. While he made an admirable effort to keep the conversation light, the atmosphere wasn't as relaxed as it could have been. Increasingly, when they were together, Lily couldn't ditch the sense of desperation she felt over him leaving.

The thought of it made her want to dig her heels in and refuse to let it happen. As though she had any control over it.

When the picnic was cleared away, Lily left Flynn loading the dishwasher and wandered back to the living room, checking for any stray dishes. Finding nothing, she went to the window and stood looking out at Porthcressa Beach.

Clouds covered the moon, and only a few stars were visible in the hazy sky. Light from the buildings along the promenade spilled out to cast shadows along the top of the beach.

Lily was in a trance when Flynn appeared behind her and sneaked his arms around her waist. Sinking into his embrace, she savoured the feel of his solid chest against her back and the distinctive scent of him that surrounded her. When his lips landed on her neck, she tilted her head and exhaled a breathy sigh.

No doubt he'd go back to his place soon. For reasons she couldn't fathom, he'd decided their relationship should go slow. Considering he was leaving in a fortnight, it seemed like a waste, but it also didn't seem to be something she could argue with without looking desperate.

"Are you okay?" he asked in her ear. "You've been really quiet this evening."

She hugged his arms against her, wishing she could pause time. "I'm okay. Thanks for the picnic."

"You're welcome." His breath tickled her ear. "I don't really want to go home."

"Don't then," she said automatically, then cursed herself for inviting a conversation she'd rather not have – about why he wanted to take things slow.

"Okay," he said instead.

She shifted, feeling the rough stubble on his chin graze against her forehead. "Okay, what?"

"I won't go home," he whispered. "If that's okay?"

A smile teased her lips, and she felt her mood lighten in an instant. Slowly, she turned and looped her arms around his neck. "What happened to taking things slow?"

His brow wrinkled. "We did that, didn't we? I've taken you on several dates where I was the epitome of a gentleman."

"That's true." She ran her fingers through the hair at the back of his head. "Somehow I just thought that the 'taking it slow' thing was going to get dragged out longer."

"I waited a week," he said, eyes sparking as he pulled her flush against him. "That's seven times longer than I'd usually go before sleeping with someone. And that week felt incredibly slow to me."

Her stomach turned a somersault. "I commend your restraint."

"You should." He kissed her slowly. "It took an insane amount of willpower."

Her smile only lasted a moment, wiped away by the intensity of their kiss.

With his willpower out of the way, months of pent-up frustration were let loose. Lily couldn't get enough of him, and the feeling was clearly mutual as they tugged at clothes and explored each other in a tangle of hands and lips and limbs.

They'd shifted to the bedroom with only their underwear remaining when a sudden noise brought Lily back into the real world.

"Is that your phone?" she asked, breathing hard.

"Yeah." He shifted slightly, his hand reaching for his discarded jeans.

"Why the heck is it so loud?"

"In case I get a call."

She squinted. "Work?"

"Yeah. We're kind of on-duty round the clock. If there are any issues during the night, we need to be available." With no luck finding his phone, he shifted to sit up and sifted through his clothes.

"I think it's in the kitchen," Lily said, eyes following the sound. "How often do you get called out at night?"

"Never." He stood and crossed the room. "But sometimes my mates call me when they're on a session. I'll shut it up."

"Hurry," Lily muttered as he left the room.

A moment later he was back and frowning at the phone, which continued to ring in his hand.

"What's wrong?" Lily asked.

"Sorry. Just a sec." He swiped his finger over the screen and moved the phone to his ear. "Sarge?"

Briefly, he closed his eyes. "A what?" He let out a small laugh. "Yeah. I thought that's what you said. I'm not at home. You can pick me up from Lily's, but we'll need to stop at my place if you want me in uniform." There was a pause while the sergeant spoke. "See you in a minute."

"What's going on?" Lily asked, sitting up to watch Flynn hastily pull his jeans on.

"I have to go," he said, snatching his T-shirt and pulling it over his head.

"I guessed that. How come?"

"Burglary." He shoved his arms into his T-shirt. Not bothering with his socks, he moved into the hallway to push his feet into his trainers.

"A burglary?" Lily asked.

"That's what the sergeant said." With a hand cupping her jaw, he kissed her. "I'm really sorry."

"It's fine," she said as he moved away.

In the doorway, he glanced back, his gaze roaming over her before he released a frustrated groan and made a dash for it.

"Flynn!" she shouted when he was halfway down the stairs.

"I'll call you later."

"Yeah, but you—" She gave up, since he clearly wasn't stopping to listen.

The living room pulsed with blue light as she walked through to peer out of the window. From there, she watched Flynn step into the police Land Rover before they sped along the promenade.

A small smile pulled at her lips as she thought of Sergeant Proctor telling Flynn his T-shirt was on backwards.

Chapter Two

Sliding into the passenger seat, Flynn caught the amused twitch of Sergeant Proctor's eyebrows, but there really wasn't time to have a conversation about his love life. Plus, for all the sergeant knew, he and Lily were just hanging out as friends. It wasn't as though it was the middle of the night or anything. They could have had dinner and watched TV.

"A burglary?" he asked, pulling his seatbelt around him. "Are you serious?"

"That's what dispatch said."

"It was a 999 call?"

The sergeant didn't slow at the junction. "We get them now and again."

"You've said that before, but I've been here for six months and I don't recall any others. It's definitely the first burglary. I'd almost forgotten that was a thing."

The sergeant put his foot down on the long stretch of road bordered by fields and hedges. "It's not usually a thing around here. Thefts of any kind are rare since it's so difficult to get away with. It's hard to get stolen goods off the island."

Flynn braced against the dashboard as the sergeant took a corner at speed.

"According to the woman who called, she disturbed them and they ran. She thought they left on foot, so there's a chance they didn't get far. Especially running in the dark."

"It feels weird without my uniform," Flynn said.

"There was no time to stop." The sergeant kept his focus on the road. "Do me a favour, though, and at least put your T-shirt on the right way before we get there."

Flynn grimaced as his gaze flicked to his chest, but he waited until they arrived at the house before pulling it off and turning it the right way.

"Your kit is on the back seat," the sarge said, stepping out of the car. "Do a sweep of the outside while I speak to the owner."

"On it," Flynn said, grabbing his radio and his belt. He switched on his torch and swept the beam over the surrounding area before striding around the side of the lone cottage to search the garden.

Only a minute passed before the sergeant came on the radio, relaying the information from the homeowner that the thief had taken off on the road heading north. Flynn told him he'd drive in that direction to look, but he wasn't optimistic about catching them given the cover of darkness and the fact that they had a head start.

Half a mile up the road, a figure sitting on the wall had him slowing to a stop.

The young, shaggy-haired guy didn't move when Flynn stepped out of the car. In the open, noise from a nearby house caught his attention, and his gaze roamed beyond the guy to the glow of a bonfire at the back of a large house.

"What are you doing sitting out here in the dark?" he asked, shining his torch beam beside the guy to illuminate him.

He squinted against the glare. "I saw flashing lights." He tipped his head the way Flynn had come. "Wondered what was going on."

"Do you live here?"

He shook his head. "Just visiting."

"But you're staying here?"

He turned, pointing over his left shoulder. When Flynn moved the beam of the torch, it landed on a small tent at the far end of the field.

"Do you know the people having a party?"

"It's an artist's retreat. They're staying in the house. I just prefer to be out in the open."

"Have you seen anyone around here this evening who shouldn't be here?"

He shook his head. "Are you a copper?"

"Yeah." Flynn frowned at the odd question before remembering he wasn't in uniform. Pulling his wallet out of his back pocket, he held out his ID to show he wasn't merely out joyriding in a police car. "PC Grainger," he said. "You are?"

"Silas." He paused before offering his last name. "Thorn."

"You haven't seen anything unusual this evening?"

"No, why?"

"I'm going to speak to the rest of your group." He hopped over the wall to take a direct route rather than continuing to the driveway. "Come with me, please." Striding through the grass, he reached for his radio and told the sergeant he was having a quick chat with the neighbours.

The wind changed as he approached, sending smoke from the bonfire rushing at him. It also carried the out-of-tune voice of the woman swaying beside the bonfire with a guitar in her hands. Apparently she kept forgetting the words but kept up a steady stream of strumming and giggling with the odd line of lyrics thrown in.

"Silas!" she said, pausing her singing but continuing with swinging her hips so her flowing white skirt swished around her legs. "Did you find a friend?"

Silas ignored the question and took a seat on a sturdy log beside a smiley middle-aged woman.

Flynn held out his ID, which got everyone's attention. "PC Grainger," he said.

"Did he really call the police on us for having a tiny little party?" The singing lady set her guitar aside and spluttered a laugh. "He's such a grump." She swung around to a man with a neatly trimmed silver beard and flat cap, lounging in a deck chair. "Didn't I tell you, Roland? I said he was looking murderous when he left earlier. I'll bet he claims it was the neighbours who complained about the noise, and not him."

"We're in the middle of nowhere," the man replied. "There are no neighbours to complain."

"Nobody made a complaint," Flynn said. "There was an incident down the road, and I wanted to ask if you'd seen anything suspicious or anything out of the ordinary."

"What kind of incident?" the lady beside Silas asked, running a hand over her frizzy blond curls.

"A break in."

"We haven't seen anyone all evening," the guitar lady said. "I'm Saffron, by the way." She stepped forward and offered her hand. "This is Roland..." She tipped her head towards the man in the deckchair and then at the two people seated on the log. "That's Martha and Silas. Best of friends, we are!" She shrieked with laughter and finally released Flynn's hand. "We actually just met a week ago, but we've bonded over our common enemy." She lowered her voice and leaned close enough that the bulky string of beads around her neck whacked against Flynn's chest. "Gideon runs the retreat, and he's a little set in his ways."

"Is he here too?" Flynn asked.

"Inside," Roland said, pushing his cap up. "He told us not to stay up late – as though we're a bunch of kids."

"He's not so bad," Martha said. "He's a very talented artist. We're lucky to learn from him." Her eyes met Flynn's. "Are the police here always so casually dressed?"

"No." He forced a smile. "Not usually. So there's nothing you can tell me? You haven't noticed any suspicious activity?"

"No." Saffron ran her finger over his upper arm. "And it's ever-so-quiet around here. If someone had come past, we'd have noticed." The scent of wine on her breath and the intrusion on his personal space had him taking a step back.

"If you think of anything, or see anything odd, please call the station." Annoyingly, he didn't have a business card to leave, but they could look the number up if need be. "And make sure you lock the doors when you go to bed."

"We can continue the party, though?" Saffron asked.

Flynn nodded. "Just keep an eye out for anything unusual."

"Want to stay and join us?" When Saffron ran a hand down his arm, he took yet another step back.

"I'm working," he said. "Enjoy the rest of your evening."

As he retreated to the road, Silas slunk away from the fire, wandering through the field and back to his tent. Saffron picked up her guitar again and continued with her dubious melody.

Flynn's radio crackled to life when he reached the car – the sergeant asking where he was.

He told him he was on his way and turned around in the driveway ahead.

Chapter Three

Hoping Flynn might return and pick up where they left off, Lily stayed awake for as long as possible. There was no word from him until she woke with a start the following morning to find a message apologising for having run out on her, and promising to call her in the morning.

She'd only been awake for ten minutes and was waiting for the toaster to pop when her phone rang.

"Morning," she said, then pushed the toast back down again when it came up too pale. "How was your night?"

"Busy."

"Yeah?" She wandered back to the living room. "There was really a burglary?"

"Two," he said. "We left one place and went straight to another call."

"Did you catch anyone?"

"No. We spent a long time looking though."

Lily sank onto the couch. "Did they take much?"

"Just some cash, a watch and a few pieces of jewellery. Whatever they could grab quickly, by the looks of it. They also robbed another house, but they went unnoticed there, so the homeowners only noticed this morning. We've just been out there."

"You really have been busy."

"Yes. This is more action than I've seen in the whole time I've been here. It's typical that it's when PC Hill is away." She could hear the smile in his voice. "I'll bet he won't be too pleased to have taken his holiday time when there's actually something to do."

"How long will he be gone?"

"Just a week. Back next Sunday."

Lily nodded, not wanting to dwell on PC Hill choosing to take his holiday time now – before Flynn left so he didn't leave the sergeant short-handed.

"Sorry for rushing off last night," Flynn said.

"Couldn't be helped," she murmured.

"You could have told me I had my T-shirt on back to front."

"I tried! You wouldn't stop to listen."

"I think the sergeant enjoyed pointing it out, anyway."

Lily chuckled. "Did he have anything to say about you being at my place and clearly having dressed in a hurry?"

"Not a lot. He seemed more amused than anything. And he suggested I have my uniform with me in the future, but I already learned that lesson after having to question people in the dark in jeans and a T-shirt. I got some strange looks, and didn't feel as confident as usual."

As she started to ask who he'd been questioning, a shrill, high-pitched tone filled the silence and demanded her attention.

Her logical brain knew immediately that the toast had burnt and set off the smoke alarm. It wasn't her logical brain that pinned her to the couch, though. Goosebumps erupted over her skin, and her pulse skyrocketed.

"Is that your smoke alarm?" Flynn asked in her ear.

Her hand with the phone sank to rest beside her, and she glanced slowly around the room, trying to make sense of her thoughts and the overwhelming sense of déjà vu.

The intense beeping of the alarm dragged her back in time. Each pause between the beeps filled her with fear.

She'd been here before – on a couch in this exact spot, as the blare of smoke alarms pulled her from sleep.

Her uncle had swept her up in the blanket she'd been asleep in and told her everything was okay. But his eyes had been filled with panic, and she'd known that everything definitely wasn't okay.

"Lily!" Flynn's distant voice pulled her from her memories, and she hurried to the kitchen, putting the phone to her ear as she went.

"I'll call you back," she said, then deposited the phone onto the kitchen table and grabbed the nearest chair to climb up and put an end to the piercing beeps.

With the alarm silenced, she opened a couple of windows and tossed the black toast in the bin. Then she fired off a message to Flynn, telling him she'd just burned her toast.

In a daze, she moved to the couch to try and untangle her memories, with no luck. Finally, she pulled herself together and got on with her day.

With her mind all over the place, the morning dragged on. A busy day was what she needed, but the trickle of customers did nothing to help keep her mind occupied.

Absently, she was wiping down tables in the middle of the afternoon when Jessica appeared beside her.

"Is everything okay?" she asked, looking at Lily with concern.

"Fine." Lily focused on her young employee. "Why?"

"I was talking to you, but you didn't seem to hear."

"Sorry." She straightened up. "I was miles away. What were you saying?"

Jessica bit her lower lip. "You won't need me in the winter, will you?"

A prickle of unease crept up Lily's spine. She'd barely needed Jessica in the past week, so she couldn't imagine winter would be different. "I guess not, but maybe we just need to come up with a new business plan for the quieter months." She glanced around the room. "Maybe we could offer kids' birthday parties... or different events..." Surely they could come up with ways to boost business and keep themselves busy. "We can have a brainstorming session sometime, but you don't need to worry – I'll find a way to keep you on."

"It's not that." Jessica shifted her weight.

A jolt of panic hit Lily as it dawned on her why Jessica looked so uncomfortable. She'd been clear from the start that she was only looking for a casual job for the summer. Considering how well it had worked out, Lily had assumed she'd stay on. She hadn't even considered her leaving.

"Are you looking for another job?" she asked. "Or have you decided on college or something?"

"No. I love working here, but I assumed it would be like most jobs on the island and you wouldn't need me over winter."

Lily smiled uncomfortably. "We'll figure something out."

Again, Jessica shifted her weight. "I appreciate it, but Rhys also won't have much work, so we were thinking we might head over to the mainland and work over there for a bit. His dad said we can stay with him in Bristol. We won't have to pay rent, so we can get jobs and save a bit of money. We thought it would be good to have six months in a city and experience something different."

"Yeah." Lily caught the gleam of excitement in Jessica's eyes. "It's a great idea," she said, pushing down her disappointment. "I bet you'll have a brilliant time."

She nodded eagerly, and her face broke into a joyful smile. "It'll be weird to live in a city, but I think it'll be fun."

"Definitely." Lily fought to keep her emotions under control. "When will you leave?"

"We were thinking maybe the end of September."

"That's only six weeks away," Lily pointed out.

"Yes. Things really quieten down around here. There'll still be some holidaymakers around in autumn, but I don't actually think you'll need me. If you want me to stay longer, I can talk to Rhys."

Lily inhaled deeply. She definitely wanted Jessica to stay longer. In fact, she didn't want her to go at all.

"Sorry," Jessica said. "Did I choose a bad time to bring this up?"

"It's fine," Lily said, blinking back tears. "You just make your plans and let me know when you'll be leaving."

"I'd really like to work for you again next year, if you'll have me back."

Lily nodded vigorously. "Whenever you want your job back, just let me know."

"Thank you." She wrapped Lily in a hug that almost made her lose control of her emotions altogether.

From the corner of her eye, Lily caught sight of Flynn walking up to the door. *Perfect timing.*

"I'll be back in a few minutes," she said, managing to smile at Jessica as she headed for the door.

Stopping Flynn with a hand on his arm, she turned him around and set off to the beach.

"Are you okay?" he asked with a puzzled expression.

"Not really," she replied.

He was leaving, and Jessica was leaving, and she definitely wasn't okay. She couldn't say that, though.

Instead, she'd stick to the problem which seemed more manageable.

"Maria definitely lied to me," she said on a ragged exhale.

Chapter Four

Even if he hadn't glanced at his watch, it was obvious Lily didn't have Flynn's full attention as she filled him in on the memories which had come back to her when the smoke alarm had gone off that morning.

"Do you need to go?" she asked before long.

"No. Sorry. Carry on..." When she failed to continue, he gestured to the sand and they took a seat. "Things are pretty hectic," he said, "so I can't stay long, but tell me about it... you really think you were staying here when there was the fire at the shop?"

"Yes. I'm sure of it."

"Why would Maria lie about that?"

"I don't know, but previously she was blasé about the fire. As soon as I brought it up, she dismissed it as not being a big deal, but it was a big enough deal for there to be a newspaper article about it. I don't believe she just forgot I was here. She lied to my face."

"Are you going to ask her about it?"

She trailed her fingers through the sand and shrugged. "I really enjoyed speaking with her about Uncle Derek. It felt as though I had a connection to him." A lump formed in her throat.

"It's not as though Maria is related to me, but she knew me when I was a kid. She feels like my only connection to my childhood, and to my family."

"You're worried you'll mess things up if you ask too many questions?"

"Yes. But that doesn't make a lot of sense. If she's lying to me, then it's not a great relationship anyway."

"Maybe she has a good reason to keep it from you."

Lily nodded. "That's what I think, but I worry I'm being too generous."

"I think it's okay to give her the benefit of the doubt."

"Uncle Derek clearly kept a lot of secrets from me," she said. "I assume he had good reasons for that, so it only seems fair I assume the same of Maria."

"Maybe she'll open up eventually," Flynn said. "She's more open with you now than when you first met, so maybe she just needs time."

"I don't want to ask her outright in case she clams up, or gets annoyed, but I can probably probe a little more without being too direct about it."

"That sounds like a good plan," Flynn said, then checked his watch again.

"Go if you need to," Lily said. "I'm fine."

"I probably should." He stood and brushed sand from his trousers.

"What's going on with the burglaries?" Lily asked. "Do you think you'll catch the culprit?"

"Hopefully. The staff at the airport and harbour are checking for anyone suspicious. But as of this morning, the thief is definitely still on the island."

"Have there been more thefts?"

He nodded. "Two backpacks were stolen from outside a cafe. And an honesty box was emptied near the community centre."

"The jam place?"

"Yes. There wasn't much cash in it, but even so the owners are upset."

"I'll bet." Lily's stomach felt suddenly heavy. She loved the honesty boxes dotted around the islands. They reflected the quaintness of the islands and the people who trusted their fellow islanders and the visitors.

"I'll talk to you later," Flynn said. "I don't know what time I'll finish though."

She nodded her understanding and pressed onto her toes to give him a quick kiss.

With no word from Flynn for the rest of the afternoon, Lily sent him a message to say she was making pasta for dinner and asked if he was joining her. An apologetic message came back to say he wouldn't be able to get away from work for a while.

The prospect of waiting around for him for the evening was unappealing, so she set off for the pub after dinner.

Seren's eyes sparkled with amusement as she looked across the bar at her. "This is an honour!"

"What's that supposed to mean?" Lily asked, sliding onto the bar stool.

"It means you haven't been in the pub much recently."

"I was here a few days ago," Lily pointed out.

"Yeah, but you sat in the corner with Flynn and ignored everyone else."

Lily's lips pulled to a smile, unable to deny it.

"I take it things are going well between you two?" Seren asked quietly.

"We've been spending a lot of time together." Lily fought a grin. "It's good."

"That's great." Seren smiled widely. "You two make such a lovely couple."

Warmth pooled in Lily's stomach but was quickly replaced

by the niggling sense of dread, which was never far away. "I don't want him to leave," she murmured.

"I know," Seren said, her eyes swimming with sympathy. "But I spoke to Sergeant Proctor the other day, and he said he's put in a request for an extra officer. It sounds as though he's been making quite a fuss about it... so you never know... maybe Flynn will end up being able to stay."

"That's what I'm hoping." Desperately, she clung to that hope, but she was also aware that it probably wasn't realistic.

"This is a terrible thing to say..." Seren leaned closer as she whispered. "But I was thinking earlier that maybe these thefts might be good for Flynn. It gives some weight to Sergeant Proctor's claims that they need another officer."

Lily grimaced.

"Yeah, I know," Seren said lightly. "I told you it's a terrible thing to say... it's not as though I'm happy about people being robbed, but if every cloud has a silver lining..." She shrugged.

"It's certainly keeping Flynn busy," Lily said, then lowered her voice. "Last night Sergeant Proctor called at a very bad time..."

Seren's eyes flashed with understanding. "I thought Flynn was insisting on taking things slow?"

"He was. But apparently we've gone slowly enough. Last night he was going to stay at my place. But then the sergeant called, and Flynn had to rush away."

She rolled her eyes. "Perfect timing."

"Yeah. And he doesn't know when he'll finish work today. With PC Hill away and all these thefts, he's busy."

Seren's eyes darted behind Lily. "Speak of the devil."

"Hi," Flynn said, the door swinging behind him as he approached Lily. "You're easy to track down."

"You could have messaged me." She checked her phone, but there was nothing from him.

"I'd offer you a drink," Seren said, eyeing his uniform, "but you don't look as though you've finished work."

"I haven't." His hand settled on Lily's back as Seren wandered away. "That's why I was looking for you. I told the sergeant I'd work late. It looks as though I'll be spending my evening driving around the island. We're hoping a visible police presence will act as a deterrent."

"Makes sense."

"I'd really rather spend the evening at your place."

She smiled weakly. "Maybe tomorrow."

His radio crackled to life, and he moved away from Lily to speak into it. "I have to go," he said a moment later. "I'll talk to you later."

The speed at which he took off gave the distinct impression that the thief had struck again.

Chapter Five

It was almost midnight when Flynn messaged to say he was only just getting home and would call Lily the next day. He didn't give much more information about his evening, other than to say that there'd been another break in but the culprit was long gone by the time they arrived.

As she got ready for her run the following morning, Lily messaged to ask if he wanted to join her. While she waited for a reply, she went to the kitchen for a glass of water, then wandered into the living room.

In the doorway, she stopped short and stifled a shriek. With her heart pounding, she raised a hand to wave at the window cleaner.

"Morning, Len," she shouted through the glass.

"Hi! Did I startle you?"

"Took a few years off my life."

"I have that effect on people," he said, the weathered skin around his eyes crinkling as he smiled. He touched a hand to his neat brown hair and gave a quick salute, then set off down his ladder.

"Creepy," Lily muttered, then felt a pang of guilt. Len was warm and cheerful and obviously loved his job.

It was the concept of unannounced window cleaners that bothered Lily. Surely it should be a job that you booked a time slot for, so you could be prepared for a face at the window, or make sure you weren't at home when they came around.

After checking her phone, she decided Flynn was probably still asleep after his late night. Jogging alone wasn't something she was used to any more, but she wanted to get a run in before she opened the shop.

Len was finishing the large windows at the front of the shop when she stepped out into the salty air. Finally, there was a bit of blue sky, but it looked set to be a blustery day.

"You're getting started early today," she said to Len.

"The early bird and all that." He worked his squeegee deftly across the large window, pressing onto his toes and stretching to reach the highest places. Barely taller than Lily, his short stature was surely a hindrance to his job. He set his squeegee in his bucket and flexed his fingers. "Making the most of the decent weather too. I'll bet this last week hasn't been good for your business either."

"It's been slow." Further along the promenade, Pippa was setting up the tables outside the cafe and waved in greeting. Both Lily and Len returned the gesture.

"Hopefully we'll get a few more weeks of good weather," Len said and idly massaged his hand.

"Are you okay?" Lily asked.

He looked confused until she nodded at his hand.

"Oh, this. A bit of arthritis. Nothing serious, but it niggles at me." After shaking his hand, he reached for his bucket and looked set to leave.

"I should get going too," Lily said. "Have a good day."

"You too!" He smiled warmly and tipped his head.

Easing into her run, she was at a slow pace at the end of the promenade when she glanced down to the vast stretch of beach. A couple of kids paddled in the shallows with their parents, and a variety of seabirds hopped along the sand while others glided on the breeze above.

Further along, a small group congregated around several picnic blankets. Artists, by the look of it. A couple of them stood in front of easels, and others sat with sketchbooks in their laps.

Lily looked out at the waves churning onto the shore and all the stunning shades of blue in the sea and sky. Boats of varying sizes broke up the smooth line of the horizon.

Paradise for artists, she thought as she followed the path and left Porthcressa Beach behind.

Running without Flynn beside her felt odd, and it occurred to her it was something she'd have to get used to. They'd probably only fit in a few more runs before he left for London. With a shake of her head, she pushed that train of thought aside. She'd deal with not having him around once he'd left, and not a moment before.

She'd see him later, so she currently had no reason for self-pity. Maybe this evening they could continue where they left off before the sergeant had interrupted them the other night. That positive thought had her smiling as she meandered along the eastern part of the island, sticking to the coast and then taking a more direct route back.

Back at the flat, she gulped down water and went straight to her phone to click into a message from Flynn, saying he'd had an early start at work but would call in on her if he could.

Setting the phone aside on the kitchen counter, her gaze snagged on the junk drawer, which was slightly open. Bumping her hip against it was ineffective, so she jiggled the assorted flyers and random items until it closed again. The cutlery drawer was open too, and she pushed it in with a frown.

In the hallway, the drawer of the console table wasn't fully closed either, and the sight of it made her pause.

For the briefest moment, she wondered whether she'd left a window open – as though a breeze might have been strong enough to open drawers.

A shiver ran up her spine as she realised she'd left the door unlocked when she'd gone on her run. Given the recent spate of crimes, she had thought about locking up, but then she'd operated on autopilot and gone with her usual routine. Apparently, she'd acclimatised quickly to island life. She almost never locked the door to the flat, and she didn't even bother too much about the door to the shop unless she'd be away for a while.

Distracted by Len, she'd forgotten her previous thoughts about locking up. Which was really stupid now that she thought about it.

With a weight tugging at her stomach, she pushed open the door to her bedroom and felt a wave of nausea – the drawer of the dresser was open and clothes were clearly disturbed. She definitely hadn't left it like that.

And the wardrobe certainly hadn't been open.

"No," she muttered, going over to it. "No, no, no."

How could she be so stupid to not lock the door?

She knew before she even looked that her backpack was gone. Of course it was. That didn't stop her from turning the room upside down looking for it.

Ten minutes later, she sank onto the bed with tears streaming down her cheeks.

All she could do was berate herself for her stupidity.

There were tens of thousands in cash in that backpack. And her passports. Two passports. One real, one a forgery. At least as far as she could tell.

She should have destroyed the fake one the moment she'd found it after her uncle died. There'd been a false passport for him too, and she hadn't hesitated in burning that one. Why had she held on to hers? Clearly, nothing good could come from it.

And now someone else had their hands on it.

She pressed a hand over her mouth as bile rose in her throat. If anyone found out she had a forged passport, it was going to raise questions she didn't have answers to. Slowly, she exhaled a breath and forced her mind to focus.

Somehow, she had to find her backpack. Preferably without letting anyone know she'd lost anything.

Chapter Six

It felt futile to lock the door now – when there was nothing of any value left – but Lily locked both the door to the flat and the front door all the same. Secondary to the stress of her missing backpack was the uncomfortable thought of someone creeping around her flat. Thinking about it gave her a chill.

Walking purposely along the promenade towards the cafe, she took deep breaths to compose herself. Hopefully, the water she'd splashed on her face before leaving had removed any trace of her earlier tears.

Crying wouldn't solve anything, and she couldn't let herself fall apart.

Several tables were occupied in The Cookie Jar, but Lily didn't pay much attention, other than to do a quick sweep for anyone she knew. As far as she could tell, it was mostly holidaymakers.

"Morning," Pippa said when Lily approached the counter.

"Hi." She ordered a black coffee and waited for Pippa to set it on the counter before she spoke again. "I don't suppose you saw anyone around the ice cream shop this morning, did you?" she asked, trying to sound casual as she handed over the exact money in coins.

"How do you mean?"

"I forgot to lock the door when I went for my run, and I had the feeling that maybe I'd had customers wandering in when the place was empty."

A crease formed between Pippa's eyebrows. "Was something missing? You know there have been some burglaries over the last few days? Flynn came in yesterday and told me to be on alert. It was mentioned on the radio this morning too."

"I know. That's probably why I got a weird feeling. Most likely it's only me being paranoid, but I thought the chairs had been moved or something... I couldn't quite put my finger on it."

"That's creepy. I saw you and Len when I was putting the tables outside, but I didn't particularly notice anyone else." Her eyes flicked across the room to where a group was just leaving, laden down with satchels and tote bags. "That guy was asking about your opening times," Pippa said quietly. "The one with the wild hair. Maybe he'd gone into the shop beforehand to see if you were open."

"Maybe," Lily mused, watching the eclectic group move outside and along the promenade.

"An odd bunch," Pippa mused while her eyes followed them. "They've been in a few times over the last week. The scruffy looking one hasn't bought a thing. Just sits there as though it's a social club."

"Who are they?" Lily asked.

"A bunch of amateur artists, on the island for a retreat. Gideon Rowe runs it. He's a bit of a recluse. Another oddball, if you ask me."

"I saw them on the beach earlier," Lily said, thinking back to the start of her run.

"Anyway. Are you okay? Are you worried someone was in the shop when you weren't there?"

Lily took a slurp of her coffee, then shook her head. "I really think I'm just on high alert and imagining things."

"That makes sense. I assume the police haven't caught anyone?"

Again, Lily shook her head. "No."

"I guess they'd be long gone by the time the police got there." She bunched her shoulders up and shivered. "You don't think about things like that happening here."

"No," Lily agreed.

"Hopefully, people will be vigilant now and this will be the end of it."

Lily finished her coffee in a long gulp. "Fingers crossed."

Stepping back outside, she glanced along the promenade and spotted the group of artists. It took her a moment to notice Flynn among them, in his uniform. Directly beside him, a tall, slim woman in a gypsy skirt and vest top laughed loudly at whatever he'd said. Leaning in, she wedged her breast against his arm and said something close to his ear. Instantly, he took a step away and directed his words to the rest of the group before leaving them behind and striding in Lily's direction.

Lost in thought, it took him a moment to spot her, but when he did, his eyes lit up in a way that gave her a momentary respite from the stress of the morning.

"I was just coming to find you!"

She smiled lightly. "Do you know those people?"

He looked over his shoulder to where the group was rounding the corner. "I met them a couple of nights ago. Some artists on a retreat or something."

"Where did you meet them?"

"They're staying close to where we were called out to for the first break in. I questioned them to see if anyone had seen anything, but they couldn't tell me anything."

Lily's brain whirred. Was it a coincidence that the group was close to one of the break-ins, and also in the vicinity when Lily had been robbed?

"Do you have any leads?" Lily asked as she ambled back towards the ice cream shop with him.

"No. The first break in was the only place where the culprit was actually seen, and the woman didn't get a look at them. Couldn't tell us anything about them, other than the direction they'd fled."

"Where was this?" Lily asked.

"Some house on its own up past the airport."

"So you don't have anything to go on?"

"Not yet. We've increased security at the ferry and the airport – keeping an eye out for anyone suspicious and spot-checking people's baggage."

Lily nodded slowly as she drew her keys from her pocket. Maybe she should tell him about the theft of her backpack. She wanted to. A problem shared is a problem halved and all that. If it were jewellery and a bit of cash, she'd tell Flynn without a second thought.

How could she explain her fraudulent passport though? And so much cash.

It would look as though she were living some sort of life of crime. Maybe that's what her childhood had been. Had her uncle been a criminal and dragged her along on whatever he'd been doing?

Blinking, she fought to focus on Flynn, and asked him to repeat what he'd said.

"I said I'm sorry we haven't been able to get any time together. It's going to be another busy day today, but do you want to do something if I finish at a reasonable time?" He shifted his weight. "You could stay at my place..."

"Sounds good," she agreed with a smile.

He squeezed her hand before heading back the way he'd come.

Feeling oddly deceitful for not confiding in him, she let herself into the shop and locked the door behind her. With another hour before Jessica arrived and not a lot to occupy her in the shop before then, Lily headed back up to the flat.

Halfway up the stairs, something crunched underfoot.

Hesitantly, she plucked the pencil from the middle of the step and turned it to read the words on the side.

Rowe Art Residency: Isles of Scilly.

Lily's heart beat faster. Apparently, it wasn't a coincidence that the artists had been in the vicinity for both burglaries.

She gritted her teeth at the realisation that one of them had stolen her backpack.

Chapter Seven

A QUICK INTERNET search gave Lily the location of the art retreat. The basic website displayed the artwork of Gideon Rowe along with information about the retreats he ran.

Too impatient to wait for Jessica to arrive, Lily sent her a brief message telling her she'd be on her own for the morning and to remember to bring her key as the front door would be locked.

A brisk twenty-minute walk brought her to the large modern house with huge windows, surrounded by sprawling fields. Wandering along the driveway, she had her sights set on the front door, but high-pitched laughter had her detouring around the side of the house.

The woman who'd been flirting with Flynn earlier stood barefoot and swinging a skipping rope in a circular motion at her side.

Nearby, the unkempt guy she'd seen in the cafe looked on with a troubled expression.

"Not like that," he said to the woman, before his eyes darted to Lily, then quickly away again.

"Hello!" the woman said. "Are you looking for Gideon?"

"Yes," Lily replied. "Is he here?"

"I don't know, but I can help you check."

"Thanks," Lily said while the woman passed the rope to the guy.

"He's been teaching me flow rope."

"Flow rope?" Lily echoed.

"Yes. It's a sort of exercise that involves swinging a rope. Silas says it has a lot of health benefits." She fell silent as the guy swung the rope while walking away from them. His movements were practised and graceful with the rope and his body moving in perfect synchrony.

"It's quite hypnotic when he does it," the woman said, then turned to Lily and thrust her hand out. "I'm Saffron, by the way."

Lily introduced herself and glanced over at the house. "Are you here on a retreat?"

"Yes. It's so much fun."

"You're an artist then?"

"Not a good one," she said with a grin. "I just love the romance of it. An opportunity came up for the ten-day retreat, and it seemed too good to turn down."

"Are you staying in the house?" Lily's gaze went to the building, which was comprised mostly of glass.

"No. That's Gideon's studio and gallery. He also has private rooms upstairs. We have accommodation over there." She pointed to what looked to be a converted barn. "It's actually nicer than I expected." Her eyes flicked to Lily. "Are you a friend of Gideon?"

"No. I don't know him. I'm interested in looking at his artwork." Her cheek twitched. That excuse wouldn't get her far. "I also have a friend in London who's thinking of doing a retreat here, so I said I'd check it out for her."

"I can definitely recommend it. Do you live on the island then?"

"Yes. I just moved here six months ago." Not even that long actually, but it felt like longer.

"Jealous!" Saffron giggled. "I'll bet it's an amazing place to live."

"I like it."

Saffron patted her arm. "Let's go and see if Gideon is around. Otherwise, I can give you a tour."

Lily followed her through the open patio door and into a huge room with white-tiled flooring, and timber support columns dotted throughout. The far end of the room was more cluttered, with cupboards and a sink, and a range of seating.

"Gorgeous, isn't it?" Saffron said. "It's such a lovely space to paint in. The lighting is fantastic."

"It's great." Lily's eyes went to the spiral staircase in the centre of the room.

"Come on," Saffron said. "Gideon is probably upstairs." She led the way up the twisting stairs to an upstairs room about half the size of the downstairs. On the far wall, paintings were stacked vertically, and on the other wall, a door was surrounded by bookcases.

"The windows are amazing, aren't they?" Saffron said, moving to look out.

"That's a lot of glass," Lily remarked, marvelling at the way the slanted roof was almost entirely windows.

"This is Gideon's personal studio. His living rooms are through here." Darting around an easel, Saffron knocked loudly on the door.

After a moment of quiet, she shrugged. "He might have gone for a walk or something. Do you want me to show you around?"

"Please," Lily said.

"If your friend wants to do the retreat, I should show you the guest accommodation," she said, heading for the stairs. "It's all on the website, of course, but the website isn't that great. Sometimes I think Gideon doesn't even want customers..." Her voice trailed off as she descended the stairs.

Instead of following, Lily moved to the door and tried the handle. The door didn't budge, and Lily briefly wondered what she'd have done if it had opened. Would she really have been bold enough to trespass?

She needed her backpack, she reminded herself. If she had to trespass to get it, so be it.

"Everything okay?" Saffron called from below.

"Sorry," Lily said, taking the steps down. "I got distracted by the view."

Saffron showed Lily more of the room below before they moved back outside.

"How many people are on the retreat?" Lily asked.

"Four. That's the maximum. That way, everyone has access to Gideon and his guidance with the art. And there are only four guest rooms."

"What's Gideon like?" Lily asked.

She lowered her voice and leaned closer. "He's pretty grumpy."

"Is he a famous artist, or something?"

"Yes!" She squinted. "I think so anyway. He used to have a gallery in London. I think he did really well for himself, but he didn't like the attention, so he moved back here for the solitude."

"Is he from here?"

"Yes. His mum was a painter too. This was the house he grew up in. He inherited it from his parents. I think that's right." Her eyes danced with delight. "Don't quote me or anything."

Lily smiled lightly. "Do you get on with the other people on the retreat? I guess that can be a bit of a gamble... it's like being on holiday with strangers."

"Weird, isn't it? I love it, though. I always enjoy meeting new people. And the people here are really lovely. I can introduce you if they're around. We'll probably leave Silas alone." Her eyes went to the guy with the rope, who was now swirling it at the other end of the field close to a tent.

"Whose tent is it?" Lily asked.

"Silas's. He didn't want to stay in the regular accommodation. I suspect he can't afford it, but maybe he also just enjoys being outdoors. It's probably both reasons."

She flicked her chin towards the building across a small patch of grass and led the way.

"I can show you my room. If you want, you can take photos for your friend." She pulled the front door open and stepped into a long hallway where the white walls displayed a selection of oil paintings which, to Lily's untrained eye, resembled chaotic swirls of colour.

"You'll just have to tell her to ignore the mess," Saffron went on.

"What?" Lily waited while she opened the first door on the right.

"If you take photos," she said with a smile. "I'm always a bit messy."

"Right." Lily followed her into the room with a double bed, wardrobe and desk.

"The bathroom is lovely and modern," Saffron said, opening the door in the corner. "The water pressure is great."

"That's good." Lily's eyes scanned the room for her backpack. Automatically, she bent down and peered under the bed, then opened the wardrobe door before realising how intrusive she was being. "My friend asked about storage space," she said. "She's one of those people who always packs too much."

"There's plenty of space," Saffron said, apparently unconcerned by Lily searching her room. "But I tend to travel light. Come on, I'll show you the kitchen and living room."

Lily stuck her head into the bathroom before following Saffron back into the hallway. They walked past more doors before arriving at the large kitchen at the back of the house. Once again, an abundance of windows offered an uninterrupted view of rolling fields.

"It's a lovely place to chill out," Saffron said.

A noise from the hallway made Lily turn.

"Hi, Martha!" Saffron called. "I'm giving guided tours now. Do you think Gideon will pay me a commission?"

"I very much doubt it," the smiley, stout lady said. She was probably in her fifties, and the soft glow on her cheeks gave her a warm presence. "I'd say you give a better tour than Gideon, though."

Lily thrust her hand out to introduce herself and repeated her story about having a friend interested in the retreat.

"I'm enjoying it," Martha said, leaning against a chair. "But I suppose it very much depends on the group. Gideon isn't actually that great at bringing people together."

"He doesn't sound very friendly," Lily said.

"He's quite serious," Martha said. "But he's a good teacher. I really think my techniques have come on in the last week."

"And you're happy with the accommodation?" Lily asked.

"Yes. It's actually nicer than the photos online."

"Are the rooms all the same?" Lily asked, desperate to get a look in all the rooms.

"I'd imagine so," Martha replied. "I don't actually know."

Lily smiled gently. "Saffron was kind enough to let me have a look at hers..."

"You're welcome to stick your head in mine, too." Martha shrugged. "You've got me wondering now... about whether the rooms are the same."

"I'd imagine they're identical," Saffron said, following Martha along the hall. "We can check the empty one too – where Silas should be staying. That one would be a good one for you to take photos for your friend."

Dutifully, Lily took photos. At least she knew no one was using the spare room to stash stolen goods. They moved from there to Martha's room.

As soon as the door was open, Lily's eyes roamed the space. Presumably, any stolen goods would be well hidden, and not just sitting out on display. The space wasn't huge though - not too many places to hide a backpack.

"Exactly the same as mine," Saffron was saying. "Except yours is much neater."

"I'm a bit of a neat freak," Martha said. "Sometimes I wish I wasn't. It doesn't seem to fit with the whole artist spirit, does it?"

Saffron leaned against the doorframe. "Maybe having a clean room leaves your mind free to be creative."

"Maybe," Martha said, chuckling. Her eyes went to Lily. "I was a primary school teacher for thirty years. Now that I've retired, I've decided to follow my passion for art. I'm not very good, but it soothes my soul to do something just because I want to."

Lily nodded while her gaze darted around the room.

"Anyway, I was just going to make a cup of tea. Would anyone else like one?"

"I'll have one," Saffron said, then looked to Lily. "Want to join us for a cuppa?"

What she wanted was to find her backpack. Fighting the urge to ransack the building, she smiled wanly. "Yes, please." She followed Saffron back into the hallway, then turned back to Martha. "I'm sorry," she said with a grimace. "Would you mind if I used the bathroom quickly?"

"Oh." Martha paused and glanced back into the room. "I suppose so."

"We'll get the tea going," Saffron called to Lily.

In the bathroom, her heart thumped wildly as she pressed her ear to the door, listening for signs that the coast was clear.

Chapter Eight

As soon as she heard Martha and Saffron's footsteps receding, Lily hurried back into the bedroom. First she checked the wardrobe, then the drawers. Her heart hammered so violently that after a moment she had to pause and force herself to breathe evenly.

There really weren't many places to hide a backpack, and she soon ran out of places to look. Crouching to peer under the bed, she spotted a suitcase and slid that out to undo the zip, but it was disappointingly empty.

Worried about being discovered, she pushed the suitcase back to its place and returned to the bathroom to flush the toilet and run the tap for a moment.

"Thanks so much," she said, joining the women in the kitchen. "You've been really helpful."

"Saffron says you live on the island," Martha remarked while pouring boiling water into three mugs. "What do you do?"

"I run an ice cream shop on the promenade."

"Oh! We were looking at that place this morning. Silas got very excited, didn't he?"

"He's a bit like an overgrown kid," Saffron said gleefully. "He really doesn't act like a thirty-year-old. Did I tell you I saw him climbing a tree the other day?"

"He's a funny one," Martha said and handed a mug to Lily.

They moved to sit at the table.

"What do you do when you're not on art retreats?" Lily asked Saffron. "Do you make money from your art?"

"Gosh, no." She grinned widely. "I'm not a proper artist – I just like trying different things. I don't have a proper career, but I always find jobs when I need them."

Martha frowned over her mug. "How did you afford this then? The retreat isn't cheap."

"I'd been staying with my aunt for a couple of months. I was saying I'd like to try my hand at painting, and she suggested I go on a retreat. She paid for it."

"That's generous." Martha's brow wrinkled. "Very lucky."

"Yes!" Saffron beamed. "To be honest, I think she might have been looking for a way to get rid of me, but I'm lucky she was willing to pay for it. My mum always says I sail through life on good luck. I think she's right – I don't know if you believe in manifesting, but it's like whatever I want, I think about it and somehow things work out."

Martha rolled her eyes, and Lily couldn't decide whether she found the notion absurd or didn't like the thought of some people getting by on luck while others have to work.

"How does the retreat work?" Lily asked. "Do you have an itinerary for your stay?"

She sipped her tea while they filled her in on the schedule, which seemed to be split between working in the studio, and out on various excursions.

After finishing her drink, Martha declared she was going for a walk before their afternoon art session.

Saffron moved to wash the mugs.

"I think I'm going to lie outside for a bit," she said, setting the last one on the draining board. "I love to lie on the ground and stare up at the clouds floating by. It's a sort of meditation."

"Sounds nice," Lily said. It also sounded like her cue to leave, unless she could come up with an excuse to hang around for longer. Inviting herself to stare at clouds with Saffron probably wouldn't be useful.

"Maybe I can check to see if Gideon is back now," she said, following Saffron to the front door.

"That's a good idea. If he's here, he'll show you his paintings. It's the only time he speaks more than a few words at a time – talking about his pictures."

A door in the hallway opened just as they were about to step outside.

"I thought I heard voices," the man with a pointed grey goatee said.

"This is Lily," Saffron said. "She has a friend interested in doing the retreat, so I've been giving her a tour. I couldn't find Gideon."

"Right." He scratched at his silver hair. "I see."

"So far I've heard glowing reports about the retreat," Lily said, taking a few steps towards him. "Are you enjoying it?"

He kept a hand on the door, his body blocking the gap between the doorframe, making it impossible for Lily to see inside. "It's good," he said curtly. "I'd recommend it."

"And you're happy with the accommodation?" Lily said. "Is your room nice?"

"Lovely." His narrow-set eyes went to Saffron. "Can I speak to you in private for a moment?"

"Of course." She patted Lily's arm. "I'll catch up with you in a second."

With a tight smile, Lily ignored the urge to barge into the guy's room and instead walked out the front door.

She lingered on the front step but had no hope of hearing what was being said inside.

A couple of minutes later, she moved aside as the door opened.

"Everything okay?" Lily asked as Saffron stepped outside.

"Yes." She shook her head. "Roland is a bit twitchy. I don't know if you heard, but there was a break in a couple of nights ago at a house down the road."

"Really?" Lily said, feigning ignorance.

"Yes. The police were here asking questions." She set off around the main house. "Roland thinks I shouldn't really be showing strangers around, given the circumstances." She spluttered a laugh. "As though you might be a burglar and you've come here in broad daylight to rob us! I told him not to be so silly."

Lily managed a small laugh. She wasn't a thief – she only intended to take back what was hers in the first place.

"It's very suspicious of him," Lily said. "What did you say his name is?"

"Roland. He's an interesting man. He worked his whole life in accounting and had his own firm and everything. Then, a couple of years ago, he gave it all up. He sold his house and car and most of his stuff and went travelling. He's been all over the world. He tells some fascinating stories."

"Amazing," Lily muttered.

"Yes. You meet really interesting people when you do stuff like this. We're all so different, but I feel very close to them. I'm hoping we'll keep in touch after the retreat." Her eyes sparkled. "It was a bit of excitement having the police here the other night. How many police officers are there on the islands?"

"Three," Lily replied. For now, anyway.

"Well..." Saffron lowered her voice. "The one who was here the other night was lovely. A young guy – probably around thirty. Dark hair and a gorgeous deep tan."

"PC Grainger," Lily stated.

"Yes. That's him! Do you know him?"

Lily nodded vaguely.

"Do you know if he's single?"

"I... umm ..." Lily did an uncanny impression of a goldfish as her mouth opened and closed. "I'm not really sure," she said.

"He's probably taken," Saffron said with a shrug. "Not that it matters. I'll be gone again in a few days. He's gorgeous, though. It might be a uniform thing too." Her eyes drifted overhead. "Look at those fluffy clouds. Just beautiful, aren't they? Maybe I'll try painting clouds this afternoon. I'll lie down and get my inspiration."

"Thanks so much for showing me around," Lily said. "I'll just nip inside and see if there's any sign of Gideon."

There was no one inside, and further snooping didn't prove helpful. Not that Lily had expected it to. Stepping back into the fresh air, she considered her options.

The backpack was close, she was sure of it. Roland had seemed shifty, and definitely not keen for anyone to see inside his room. Which could mean he's hiding something or just that he's a private person... or it could mean nothing at all.

The locked door up in Gideon's studio had Lily itching to get inside and look around too. Her eyes went to the tent at the far end of the field. Silas and his rope were nowhere to be seen. Lily's impression of him didn't give her any suspicious vibes, but she also hadn't really spoken to him.

A tent shouldn't be hard to get access to for a quick root around.

She needed to come back when no one was here. With the place to herself, she could do a thorough search. Briefly, she pondered what lengths she'd go to in order to get her backpack. Would she break the law herself? Breaking in to retrieve what was hers didn't seem that immoral to her. The problem was knowing exactly where to strike. If she knew for definite who had her stuff, she wouldn't think twice about breaking in.

Besides, she couldn't imagine a thief would report the loss of stolen goods.

"Did you find him?" Saffron called, breaking Lily from her thoughts.

"No. I might try again tomorrow."

"We'll be out on an excursion to Tresco Abbey Garden in the morning, but we'll be here in the afternoon."

"Thanks." That was good to know.

On the walk back to Hugh Town, a constant prickle of anxiety plagued Lily, and her thoughts wouldn't slow down. Certain she'd be no use in the ice cream shop, she didn't return directly but wandered aimlessly.

Or so she thought. The fact that she ended up outside the police station would suggest it wasn't so aimless after all.

She pressed her lips together as she stared at the grey building, wishing she could go inside and tell Flynn everything. She'd feel better if she could confide in someone.

Not just someone – in Flynn.

Emotions caught in her throat.

She couldn't share this with Flynn. Thanks to her uncle, she had to deal with it alone.

Chapter Nine

THE SIGHT of Lily outside the station brought an instant smile to Flynn's face. She hadn't noticed the police car, and he put the window down to call out to her, but paused at the haunted look on her face. His smile fell away as a ripple of fear crept up his spine.

Something was wrong.

"Lily!"

Her head shot up, and the sadness that had been there vanished so quickly he wondered if he'd imagined it.

"Looking for me?" he asked.

"Yeah," she replied, stepping into the road with a smile so unnatural he knew for sure there was a problem.

"What's wrong?"

"Nothing. Why?"

"Because you look..." He shrugged. Maybe he was imagining things. "Hop in," he said, reaching across to open the passenger door. "I can drop you home."

"Thanks."

"Busy morning?" she asked while she pulled her seatbelt around her.

"Yes. I take it you heard about the latest break-ins?"

"No. What happened?"

"I assumed you wanted the inside scoop." He raised an eyebrow. "But you just wanted to see me?"

"Yes," she said, and the heat colouring her cheeks made him wonder what exactly was going on with her. "How many more break-ins have there been?"

"Two more this morning. All the properties had their doors unlocked. Someone's taking advantage of the islanders' trusting nature. We're putting out alerts for people to be vigilant and lock their doors."

"Where were the break-ins?"

"One on Church Street, and one on Buzza Street. Near your place, actually. You haven't seen anyone suspicious, have you?"

She shook her head. "Do you have any leads?"

"So far, no one has seen anything. Whoever it is has a talent for going unnoticed. We've also had a few people report missing jewellery. Just odd pieces, so they thought it was lost, but since the reports of the break-ins they're now suspecting they might have been stolen."

"I guess an item of jewellery or two could easily go unnoticed. That's pretty sneaky."

"Yeah." He pulled over on the street behind the promenade.

"Are you allowed to use the police car as a taxi?"

"No. Definitely not." He grinned. "Don't tell on me, will you?"

She looked lost in thought. "I had a weird conversation today," she said, then fell silent again.

"Are you going to tell me about it?" he asked when she looked as though she'd lost her train of thought.

Her cheeks flushed again. "It was kind of stupid, but this woman was asking me about you... wanted to know if you were single..."

His eyebrows drew together. "Which woman?"

"Oh." She grimaced. "She's on an art retreat. Saffron. She mentioned she'd met you."

"I think I know who you mean. Where did you meet her?"

Her mouth opened and closed a couple of times before she spoke. "At the ice cream shop."

"She's one of the group I met the other night. I think she was flirting with me. Or maybe she's one of those people who flirt with everyone."

"No. I think it was just you."

"And she wanted to know if I'm single?" he asked, lifting an eyebrow.

"Yeah."

"What did you say?"

She shrugged. "That I didn't know."

A laugh escaped him. "You don't know?"

"I mean..." She shifted in her seat. "I just didn't know what to say..."

His stomach dropped. Maybe this was why she was acting so oddly. "Are you annoyed with me because I said we should take things slow?"

"No," she said unconvincingly.

"It had nothing to do with my feelings for you," he said, the words feeling clumsy and awkward. "I was trying to be romantic... and just..." He swallowed hard. "Just not rush things. But I definitely..." He paused and cleared his throat. "As far as I'm concerned, you can tell people I have a girlfriend. That's what I'd tell people. If that's okay with you?"

"It's okay with me," she said with a subtle nod.

"You could look happier about that," he teased.

"I'm happy about it."

He wanted to point out that she looked anything but happy, but since she didn't seem to be in the mood to chat, he wasn't sure there was much point.

"Do you still want to do something tonight?" she asked.

"I'd love to, I'm just not sure what time I'll finish."

"Yeah, of course. We can do something tomorrow."

"I wasn't saying no to tonight," he said quickly. "Hopefully, I won't need to work too late, but the sergeant isn't feeling great, so I'm trying to take up the slack. Also, if I manage to finish at a decent time, could you come to my place? If this thief strikes again, I need to be ready to go."

"Let's just leave it for tonight," she said, a vacant look in her eyes. "It'll only stress you out trying to get out of work in time."

"It's fine," he said, confused. "Also, I wanted to talk to you about my flight."

"What flight?"

He blinked a couple of times. "My flight back to the mainland. When I leave..."

"What about it?"

"I booked it." He'd put it off for as long as possible, as though that might change things.

"Okay." She let out a sigh. "Why do you want to talk to me about it?"

"I thought you might like to know when it is?"

"Soon, I imagine. A couple of weeks, right?"

He nodded slowly. "A week on Saturday." Just less than a fortnight. Two weeks today, he'd be back in London.

"The sergeant might still be able to pull some strings and make your job here permanent."

"He's trying," Flynn said. "And I actually think he'll manage it, but these things move slowly, so I can't imagine it happening in the next two weeks." He'd been hoping so, but that hope was pretty much dead now.

"I'll still keep my fingers crossed." Lily leaned over and gave him a kiss that was all too brief. "I'll talk to you later."

She hopped out of the car so fast that he was fairly sure she didn't even hear him call goodbye.

He'd been hoping that telling her about his flight would be a dose of reality that would get them talking more seriously about their future plans.

At least he'd put it out there. Maybe she just needed time for it to sink in, and he'd get more out of her later.

Or maybe she'd continue to bury her head in the sand about him leaving.

Chapter Ten

ASSUMING the group of artists would get one of the day tripper boats to Tresco, Lily loitered at the harbour, hoping the cap shading her face didn't make her look conspicuous. She dipped her head when she saw the group arrive and file onto the ferry. Glancing up, she did a quick head count to make sure no one had stayed behind, then set off for a walk across the island.

Knowing there was no one home, she didn't hesitate in striding down the drive towards the guest accommodation. Instinct had her wanting to check out Roland's room first. Plus, she had an inkling it would be easier to find a way into their accommodation. If the doors were locked, maybe she could find a window open.

Eager for a chance to recover her backpack, she broke into a slow jog as she rounded the house.

The figure at the back made her stop short, though he looked even more startled than she was.

"Len!" she gasped.

Laughing, he pressed his palm into the centre of his chest. "You almost gave me a heart attack!"

As her pulse settled down, she frowned. "What are you doing here?"

"Working!" He waved his squeegee in the air. "What are you doing here?"

She looked up at the house with its abundance of windows. "I suppose there's quite a bit of work for you here."

"You can say that again. And apparently Gideon needs perfect light to work in, so I'm here every few weeks. Which I wouldn't mind if he'd compensate me properly."

Lily's frown deepened.

"Especially given how much he charges for letting people stay and paint with him," he went on. "You'd think he'd pass some of that on to me."

"Surely you could refuse to come unless he pays more?"

"He reckons he can get someone else to do it for what he pays me. No idea if that's true, but I don't seem to be in a strong position to negotiate. Anyway, I'm yapping away as usual. What are you doing out this way?"

"Looking for Gideon?" Lily said. "Is he around?"

"No. Won't be back until this afternoon. Which means I get to work in peace. He drives me crazy when he stands beside me, looking at me as though I've no idea what I'm doing."

"Sounds frustrating," Lily said. "How long does it take you to do all this?"

"The downstairs will take me an hour or two. I've a lad coming to help me with the upstairs windows. Can't manage them alone. I said I'd mow the lawn while I'm here as well."

"Here for a while then," Lily glanced around as she attempted to come up with a new plan. "You don't have a key, do you?" she asked hesitantly, then kept talking when he didn't immediately reply. "I've been wanting to have a look through his paintings. I was here yesterday, and I missed him then as well. It looks as though I've made another wasted trip today."

"You should probably try calling first next time."

"That's a sensible idea," she said.

"I don't have a key," he said when Lily had just about given up on him answering the question. "A lot of people give me keys.

Sometimes they want me to clean the insides of the windows, or have some other odd jobs for me. Not Gideon. If I clean the inside, it's always when he's here and with him looking over my shoulder like a hawk."

"Annoying," Lily muttered.

"I can tell him you called by, if you'd like."

"That's fine, thanks. I'll give him a call and arrange a time to come back."

"It's weird, you know."

"What is?"

"His artwork. Costs a small fortune, and it's very weird – just paint splatters on a canvas. I'm not convinced he ever sells any of it. Just makes his money from the retreats as far as I can tell."

"I've heard good things about his paintings and wanted to have a look. My walls are looking a little bare."

"Pay me no mind," he said jovially. "Everyone's taste is different, and I certainly don't know much about art. Only know what I like and what I don't. Now, back to work for me!"

"Me too," she said, with a sinking feeling in her stomach.

Failing to come up with another plan, she wandered back the way she'd come, only to stop a little further down the road as she caught sight of the tent close to the large oak tree at the end of the field. Her eyes drifted to the house, gauging whether Len could spot her from this distance. Given the slant of the landscape, she suspected she'd go unnoticed if she kept to a crouch.

She'd give it a go anyway since she couldn't face going back to the shop having made no progress. With any luck, Len would be focused on his work and wouldn't even glance in her direction.

The crouched run was a solid workout, but the fear of getting caught and the hope of retrieving her belongings overshadowed her burning quads.

At the entrance to the tiny one-man tent, she kept low and made quick work of dragging the zip open. The smell hit her immediately – a pungent mix of sweat and damp air that had her nose twitching in protest and made her question whether the search was really necessary. Even though she'd only met him briefly, she'd got no suspicious vibes from Silas. Maybe because he came across as someone who didn't place money and material possessions high on their list of necessities.

Kneeling at the entrance to the tent, she took hold of the hiking backpack blocking her way and had a quick root through it but only found a few sets of clothes and a wash bag. There wasn't much else to search. She disturbed what appeared to be a small pile of washing, then leaned further into the humid tent to pat down the bedding and pillow. Nothing there, just as she'd suspected.

At least she could cross Silas off her list of suspects.

For the rest of them, she'd either have to come back later and poke around while they were all here, or tomorrow – which suddenly felt like forever away.

Chapter Eleven

She should have gone back to the shop to give Jessica a hand, but as she wandered past the airport, she had the bitter notion that she should make the most of her freedom while she could. Before long she wouldn't have Jessica to take care of the shop for her. She wouldn't be able to come and go as she pleased.

Arriving at Glynis's house, she didn't hesitate on the doorstep, but gave a short, loud knock on the wooden door.

"Hi," Maria said, answering it a moment later. "How are you?"

Lily opened her mouth to say she was fine, but the words got stuck in her throat. "I don't know," she said limply. "Do you have time for a chat?"

Smiling warmly, she stepped aside to let Lily in.

"Is Glynis here?" Lily asked, following her through to the kitchen.

"No. She's out for lunch with a couple of friends. Can I get you a drink?"

Lily accepted a glass of water, and they moved out to sit on the patio. The neatly manicured lawn and bright flowerbeds should have been calming, but Lily's thoughts continued to race.

"Jessica's leaving," she told Maria after a few minutes of companionable silence.

Maria set her glass on the table. "The girl who works for you?"

"Yes." Lily chewed on the corner of her thumbnail. "When she started working for me, it was only supposed to be a temporary thing, so I don't know why it feels like a surprise... but this week she told me she's going to spend the winter on the mainland. She's leaving in September."

Maria nodded. "She's doing you a favour. You won't need an employee over the winter, and it saves you the uncomfortable conversation of telling her that."

"I'd have kept her on," Lily said.

"You'll barely make any money. If you're paying staff over the winter, you'd be running at a loss."

"So I'd run at a loss for a few months."

Maria smiled sympathetically. "There'd also be nothing for her to do. She'd be bored stiff. It's good that she's going to the mainland for a while."

Lily shook her head as a surge of irritation hit her.

"*You* could plan on having a holiday in the winter," Maria went on. "That's what I used to do. Just close completely for a couple of months and get away for a while."

Lily's mind went to a conversation she'd had with Flynn about spending time in London with him. Her chest tightened at the thought. "I don't want to go anywhere," she said through gritted teeth.

Maria shifted in her seat. "It's up to you, of course. But expect things to be much quieter here."

"I wish we'd stayed here," Lily said, the words taking her by surprise.

Maria's eyebrows rose questioningly.

"I wish Uncle Derek hadn't dragged me off to Italy after my parents died. If he wanted to be with you, he should have stayed here."

The sorrow in Maria's eyes should have been enough for Lily to leave the conversation alone, but the anger simmering in her veins wouldn't settle.

"Why did we leave?" she asked, desperate to know if Maria knew more than she'd been letting on.

"I guess Derek thought it was for the best."

"It doesn't make sense," Lily snapped. "He wanted to be with you... and I understand he thought a change of scene would be good for me... but why not stay here? This is the perfect place to raise a child. Why did he feel the need to take me to a country where I couldn't speak the language?"

"He had the job offer..."

"Which he presumably applied for," Lily put in. "That didn't just come out of nowhere, did it?"

"No, but he'd always been someone who liked to move around..."

"Really?" Lily asked, her tone softening.

Maria nodded. "That's how I met him, remember?"

"Yes," Lily mused. So it wasn't only after he'd taken custody of her that he'd felt the need to constantly be on the move.

"He always loved seeing different places," Maria said. "I suppose he wanted you to experience different cultures too."

Lily nodded. "I was thinking it must have been upsetting for him when there was a fire at your shop so soon after my parents' fire." She let the words hang in the air, waiting to see how Maria would respond.

The small twitch of her cheek and the flash of panic in her eyes would have gone unnoticed if Lily hadn't been paying attention.

"I'm not sure he even knew about it," she said, clasping her hands in her lap.

"Did it happen before we came to stay or after we'd left for Italy?" Lily asked bluntly.

Maria shook her head as though trying to get her thoughts in order. Or more likely, trying to keep up with her own lies.

"After you'd left," she said. "But the fire in the shop wasn't a big deal."

"Big enough that there was a newspaper article written about it," Lily pointed out.

"It didn't exactly make the national news," Maria said, sinking back into her seat and seeming to relax. "It was a lot of fuss about nothing."

Lily swallowed hard, not sure what her next move should be. Should she tell Maria she remembered being in the shop when it happened? Demand to know why she was lying, and what secrets her uncle had been keeping from her?

"Are you okay?" Maria asked softly. "You seem agitated?"

"I'm angry with Uncle Derek for dying and leaving me with so many unanswered questions," she said sulkily. "And I guess it upset me when Jessica said she was leaving."

"Just Jessica?" Maria probed.

Lily winced. Of course it wasn't only about Jessica leaving. Flynn was leaving too – but that hurt too much to talk about.

"Sorry," Lily said, standing abruptly. "I shouldn't have come."

"You're always welcome here," Maria said. "I'm only sorry I can't be more helpful."

Lily shrugged, suspecting Maria *could* be more helpful. She just chose not to be.

Chapter Twelve

Maybe she should have been more direct with Maria. Stopping in the middle of the deserted lane, Lily contemplated turning and marching back there to accuse her of lying about the fire. She could also ask her outright if she could explain why Uncle Derek had kept forged passports for the two of them, and enough cash to disappear without a trace.

Was it to do with Lily and her parents, or did he have a shady past that predated him becoming guardian to his niece?

"Are you okay?"

Lily's mind returned to the present. Glynis stood before her.

"You look pale," the old lady said, resting a comforting hand on Lily's arm. "Are you feeling okay?"

"I was visiting Maria," she said, glancing back towards the house.

"That's nice. It's good that you two are getting to know each other properly."

"Yes." Lily gave a small shake of her head, clearing away her previous thoughts. "How was your lunch?"

"Very enjoyable. I met up with Mirren Treneary. It's been ages since I had a proper natter with her."

"She's lovely," Lily said automatically. Her mind went to the first time she'd met the warm, local woman. She'd been trying to track down the owner of the ice cream shop, and Mirren had given her the name.

Lily's eyes snapped to Glynis as it occurred to her that it wasn't only Maria who might give her information.

"What's that look for?" Glynis asked suspiciously.

"I know you hate talking about Maria behind her back," Lily said. "But I still can't figure things out. I don't know if Maria can't remember, or if she's purposely keeping things from me..."

"Why would she do that?" Glynis asked.

"I don't know." Lily pressed her lips together. "You told me that Maria had an old friend here to visit. Now I know that was my uncle, and I was with him. But I need to know if I was here when there was a fire at the ice cream shop. Do you remember if Maria had visitors at the time?"

"Not that I recall."

"Surely you'd remember if she had," Lily mused, more to herself than Glynis.

She blew out a breath. Maybe Maria had been telling the truth. Perhaps her memories of being here at the time weren't real. Or maybe it was something different. It could well be that it was only burnt toast that had set off the smoke alarm when Lily was a kid.

"What's going on, Lily?" Glynis asked.

"Nothing. My mind is playing tricks on me. Ignore me." She forced a smile. "Enjoy the rest of your day."

Leaving Glynis, she walked with an urgency that had her breathless by the time she marched up the path to the front door of Mirren Treneary's house.

Surprise must have been clear on her features when it was Denzel who opened the door rather than Mirren. It took her a moment to remember that the local landscape gardener was dating Mirren.

"I assume from that look it's not me you're after?" he said.

"No. Hi."

"Hey." He turned back to shout into the house that Lily was here, then stepped outside. "I was just leaving. Got to get back to work."

"Nice to see you," Lily murmured, then stepped inside and followed Mirren's voice to the kitchen.

"This is a nice surprise," Mirren said, crossing the room to hug her.

"Does Denzel live here now?" Lily asked, glancing through the large window to watch him stride to his truck.

"Not officially. He still has his own place, but he's here most of the time now that we're not hiding things any more."

"That's nice."

"It is," Mirren said with a bright smile.

Lily declined a drink and took a seat at the kitchen table. "I wondered if I could ask you some more questions about Maria."

Mirren scratched the bridge of her nose. "Who?"

Lily gave a small shake of her head. "Gail Greenway. The owner of the ice cream shop."

"Of course." Mirren rolled her eyes. "That's a funny business if you ask me. Glynis was actually filling me in on it at lunch today. But I also bumped into Maria at the supermarket the other day, and she said hello. I wouldn't have recognised her, but she explained that she goes by her middle name now." She sighed. "Said she had a mid-life crisis years ago and felt like a change."

"It is a little odd," Lily said. "She knew my uncle. I don't know if Glynis told you that."

"She didn't," Mirren said, her brow furrowed. "Why didn't Maria mention that to you earlier? What was all the secrecy for?"

"It was a long time ago that she knew him," Lily said defensively. "I really don't think she meant any harm."

Mirren gave a one-shouldered shrug. "What did you want to ask me?"

"I wondered if you remembered much about the fire at the ice cream shop?"

Again, she shrugged. "I remember Gail – sorry, Maria – being shaken up. A few of us pitched in to clean the place up."

"And there was only Maria there at the time of the fire? She didn't have friends staying or anything?"

"No. I'd remember that."

"Are you sure? It would have been a man with a child?"

Mirren looked briefly as though she was going to ask questions of her own, but thought better of it. "Definitely not," she said. "I wasn't there at the time of the fire – Kit was still little, so I stayed at home with him, but Terry went down to help."

"Your husband? He went to help with the fire?"

She nodded. "Terry was a volunteer firefighter. He got the call and went straight down there. I'd have known if there had been a child staying there. I'd remember something like that."

"Yes, I suppose you would." Which meant Lily must have got it wrong.

She scrubbed her hand over her face. It should have been a relief that Maria hadn't been lying, but she still felt she was missing some fairly large pieces of the puzzle. Ones that would explain her forged passport.

The thought of it made her stomach lurch. She needed to stop focusing on twenty-year-old fires and put her attention on retrieving her stolen items.

"Sorry," she said to Mirren, feeling slightly dazed as she stood. "I didn't mean to disturb your afternoon."

"You didn't." Mirren followed her to the door. "Are you okay?"

Lily nodded. That was all she could manage.

The gesture didn't convey the truth in the slightest.

Back at the shop, Lily sent Jessica for a late lunch break. She tried to concentrate on customers while her brain whirred over her next move for tracking down her backpack. The only thing she could come up with was to head back to the art retreat after the shop closed and use the excuse of speaking to Gideon about his paintings.

It turned out, all the time spent mulling over her next move was for nothing. Gideon Rowe called the ice cream shop in the middle of the afternoon.

"Len Marrack said you want to look at my paintings," he said down the phone – straight to the point, no small talk. "I'm back at the studio now and will be available to show you my paintings for the next couple of hours if that would suit you."

Lily stammered a little before saying that would be fine and she'd be over shortly. With Jessica more than happy to be left alone again, Lily didn't bother waiting until closing time.

She was halfway to Gideon's place when her phone rang. Flynn's name flashing on the screen didn't bring the usual sense of joy, and she found herself hesitating to answer. In the end, she couldn't bring herself to ignore the call.

"What have you been up to today?" he asked cheerfully.

"Not much. Just working."

"Oh."

"Why?"

"No reason." He sounded oddly unsure of himself. "I called in at the shop," he said after a brief pause.

"When?"

"Before lunch. Jessica said you were out somewhere, but she wasn't sure where..." He trailed off. "And now it sounds as though I'm checking up on you."

"Jessica must have forgotten to mention you stopped by, otherwise I'd have called you. I actually went to visit Maria."

"How was that?"

"Uneventful."

"Did you ask her about the fire again?"

"Yeah. She said Uncle Derek and I had already moved to Italy. So I guess I was imagining things that didn't actually happen."

"I can't imagine it's as simple as that. Maybe Maria was lying."

"I don't think so, because I also asked Glynis and Mirren if they remembered someone staying with Maria at the time of the fire. I'm sure they'd remember if a child had been there."

Even in the silence, she could feel his sympathy.

"Things seem a little quieter here," he said eventually. "I can wander over to the shop for a bit."

"Don't," Lily said, then cursed herself. "I mean, don't feel you have to. I'm fine, and I need to do some shopping, so I might not even be around." It wasn't technically a lie. Just that the implication was she'd be food shopping and not pretending to shop for artwork.

"Are you annoyed with me?"

"No," she said impatiently. "Why would I be?"

"Because you were upset about Maria and I didn't have time for you, and—"

"You did have time for me," she said, cutting him off. "You sat on the beach and listened to me when you should have been at work."

"Yes, but..."

"I'm not annoyed with you," she said, forcefully this time.

"Okay. Well, I want to hear all about it later."

"Thanks," she muttered. "Is there anything new concerning the burglaries?"

"No. It seems as though the thief went on a spree and then stopped. Which makes sense since they've lost the element of surprise – people are being more careful about security."

Lily suspected the real reason was that they'd decided they'd hit the jackpot with her backpack and could retire from their life of petty crime.

"We've got people on the lookout for anyone suspicious leaving the islands by sea or air," Flynn went on. "So we should still have a good chance of catching them."

"Fingers crossed." She smiled at the young woman pushing a

buggy and waved at the little one, who she knew was partial to her banana ice cream.

"Hi, Lily!" the toddler said, waving madly.

"Hello," she cooed in return.

"I should let you get on," Flynn said. "You sound busy."

Grimacing, she told him she'd talk to him later before ending the call.

Chapter Thirteen

"THAT WAS a spot of bad luck that you didn't catch me this morning," Gideon said, plodding up the spiral stairs ahead of Lily. "At least Len finally came in useful, even if it was passing on messages."

Lily stepped up into the art studio, which was flooded with afternoon sunlight. "I'd imagine keeping your windows clean is pretty helpful too."

"Yes, but the attention to detail isn't always what it could be." He pointed to the corner of the window. "Look at that streak."

Lily pursed her lips as she fought to make out the tiny smudge at the very edge of the pane. It was on the tip of her tongue to suggest he should pay him more if he wanted a better service, but she kept the thought to herself.

"I believe you've got some paintings to show me," she said instead.

"I have." He moved to the end of the room, where canvases leaned against each other like tightly packed dominoes. "I'll be honest, I've been into your ice cream shop, and I have to say I'd never have thought you the type to be interested in high-quality artwork."

"It's not for the shop. I keep the decor purposely generic downstairs. I'm looking for something for my flat."

"It seems I misjudged you, that's all. I suppose I've just got used to the locals not appreciating my art. They all want stuff that looks like photos of local scenery. Makes no sense to me. If you want something that looks like a photo, take a photo!" He rolled his eyes beneath his thick dark eyebrows and tugged at his brightly coloured neckerchief. "I used to have a studio in London, you know. In the heart of the art scene. It's a different life when you're surrounded by people who appreciate your talent."

"What made you move back here?"

"In the end, city life wasn't for me. I need tranquillity to create. I get that here."

"Absolutely," Lily said, looking pointedly out of the window.

"Anyway, I don't know if you've looked at my collection online..."

"I had a little look."

"My personal favourites are the ones of the local landscapes." He began poring through the paintings. "Somewhere here I have one of the view from Porthcressa Beach which might take your fancy given it's your neck of the woods."

Lily actually wouldn't mind a nice seascape, despite the fact that she only needed to look out of the window for the real thing.

"Here we go." He pulled out a large square canvas with several thick swaths of yellow and some chaotic blue and black squiggles.

Tilting her head, she wondered which way up you were supposed to look at it to see the view from Porthcressa Beach. Maybe it was like those magic eye pictures where you had to squint a certain way.

"My interpretation of the view, of course."

"Hmmm." She fought for words. "Fascinating," she murmured.

"Thank you."

"Could you show me some more?"

"Yes, yes." His eyes sparkled, and she felt a pang of guilt for making him think he had a chance of a sale.

As he showed her more of the same in varying colours, she nodded and murmured appreciative words.

"It's hard to choose," she said eventually. Moving to the window, she tried to give the air of pondering, but her eyes drifted to the door among the bookshelves, and she was suddenly desperate to get into his private rooms. "I wonder if you have anything else," she said, as an idea hit her.

"How do you mean?"

"I saw all these pictures on your website. And while they really are special, I wonder if you have anything that you don't put on general display." She wrinkled her nose. "Those pieces artists create purely for themselves and keep hidden away."

He hesitated long enough for Lily to think she'd taken the wrong tack.

"Maybe there is something." A muscle in his cheek twitched as he withdrew a single bronze key from his pocket. "Wait here and I'll have a look."

"I can come with you," Lily insisted, hot on his heels as he unlocked the door.

"No." His voice was commanding, and he turned and pulled himself to his full height – a head taller than Lily. "Please wait here. I'll just be a moment."

With the door being closed in her face, Lily wanted to get inside even more badly. Surely people with nothing to hide didn't slam doors in people's faces. Or even just shut doors firmly after politely requesting people wait.

Lily wasn't great at waiting. Or at doing as she was told.

Not when she was investigating, anyway.

After a couple of minutes, she pushed the handle and stepped inside. Confused by what she saw, she didn't get very far.

In contrast with the other rooms in the house, there was no

neatness and order. Books and magazines were stacked against every wall in the small hallway. She spotted two vacuum cleaners and a toolbox amid assorted furniture that had no business being in the hall.

"I said wait out there." Gideon appeared with a couple of small frames under his arm and ushered her back the way she'd come. He sounded more embarrassed than anything. "It's a mess, I know. I'll get to it eventually, but for now I just keep the door locked so no one has to see it."

"That's a lot of stuff." Her mind tried to untangle things. That could have been his horde from any number of burglaries, but somehow she got the feeling it was more like a lifetime's worth of accumulated junk.

"When I converted the place for the retreats, I shoved all my personal items up here out of the way, to keep a minimal vibe for the retreat. But there's too much for the space, and I know it looks like junk, but a lot of it holds sentimental value, and I can't bring myself to get rid of it."

"I didn't mean to intrude," she said weakly, though that was exactly what she'd intended.

"Anyway." Gideon pulled the door closed behind them, leaving them in the bright and calm studio. "I wouldn't usually show these to anyone, but you seem to appreciate my style of art, so I'll let you have a look. They are a little different from my usual style. I'll warn you of that."

She drew in a steady breath as he turned the paintings to show her. To be fair, they differed from the other paintings, but as far as Lily could tell, only in the colour scheme. What with these being black and grey rather than the brighter colours.

"It gives the sense of a storm," Lily said.

"Precisely. I knew you'd get it. Not a storm in the literal sense, though."

"Of course not," Lily chimed, as though she had a clue what on earth they were talking about.

"I knew you'd like these." He held one up and gazed at it.

"That's partly why I was hesitant to show you. I'm not sure I can part with them, you see."

"I can understand that." Lily really didn't want him to part with them either.

"I'm sorry if I got your hopes up, but I don't think I could even put a price on them. What about the one of Porthcressa Beach? I'd do you a little discount on that one. The online price is six thousand pounds, but I could knock off a couple of hundred for you."

Her throat spasmed, and it was an effort not to choke.

"I'll have to think it over. I'd need to measure the walls too."

"It's because you've seen these, isn't it?" He sighed as he looked lovingly at the paintings in his hands.

"Gideon!" a female voice called before Saffron appeared at the top of the stairs. "We're all downstairs waiting for you."

"Whatever for?" he sniped.

"The charcoal workshop."

"That's not until four o'clock."

"It's four now." Saffron thrust her watch out as proof.

"Well, I'll be down shortly. I'm just in the middle of a meeting."

Saffron smiled. "Hi, Lily."

"Hi. Have you had a good day?"

"Excellent, thank you. I'm just excited to learn about working with charcoal now. Roland tells me it's his speciality." Her smile vanished. "I mean… I'm sure he's not as good as Gideon, but it's his favourite type of art, so he's got me all excited."

"I was just going anyway, so I'll leave you to get on with it."

If only there were a way for her to sneak into the guest accommodation while they were all busy with their charcoal lesson. The fact that every wall downstairs was comprised mostly of glass would make that fairly difficult.

She waved to the group as she exited through the French doors and only then noticed that the retired schoolteacher was sitting on a large log by the unlit fire pit. Lily fought to remember her name as she approached from behind her.

Martha.

She only realised she was on the phone at the last minute, and Martha was so focused on the conversation that she didn't register Lily.

"I can't figure out how to switch it to a video call," she was saying, with the phone pressed to her ear. "I'm trying, but I can't get it to work. I don't know what's wrong with it."

"Need some help?" Lily asked.

Martha's fierce gaze whipped around to Lily, but she only clutched the phone more tightly as she stalked away.

"I'll take that as a no then," Lily muttered.

Chapter Fourteen

THE PROCESS of making ice cream usually soothed Lily, but it seemed there was nothing that would help her frayed nerves that evening. Her tension was evident in the way she jumped when the bell above the door jangled.

Sticking her head around the door frame, she caught Flynn's eye.

"You should keep the door locked," he told her with a reprimanding look.

"I will when I go upstairs, but I don't think anyone is going to steal anything when I'm right here." Besides, they'd already robbed her – she couldn't imagine them coming back for another go.

She went back to adding crumbled ginger biscuits to the caramel ice cream.

"You're still on duty," she said when Flynn leaned against the counter to watch her.

"Yes." He grimaced.

"I take it you're not available to hang out again this evening?"

"Sorry. We need a visible police presence, and the sergeant offered to do it but he had this weird dizzy spell earlier."

"Is he okay?"

"He says he's fine, but I think he's actually ill and trying to battle through. He didn't argue when I offered to work again this evening, so that's a sure sign he's not 100 percent fit."

Slowly, Lily began folding the biscuits into the mix.

"Sorry," Flynn said, apparently misinterpreting her silence as annoyance at him.

"It's fine."

He stood up straighter. "Tomorrow evening I'm all yours, I promise."

"Glad to hear it," she said, forcing positivity into her voice.

"I can also take a quick dinner break this evening, so I thought I could grab us a takeaway and you can tell me all about your conversation with Maria before I head off on patrol."

"Or I could go on patrol with you," she suggested. That way she'd be around to retrieve her backpack if he caught the thief.

His instant grimace was an obvious answer. "I'm not really allowed to do that..."

"Yeah, of course."

"Sorry," he said again.

"Don't worry about it. Stupid idea." What were the chances he'd catch anyone, anyway? The police didn't have any leads. As far as she could tell, she was still more likely to find the culprit before they did.

If she didn't...

She stopped her stirring and stared up at Flynn.

Maybe she should tell him. If the police found the stolen goods before she did, it would be good if he knew. She could explain that she didn't know where Uncle Derek had got the passport from, or why. Same with the money.

It would put Flynn in a tough position, though. He'd have to report it. She could hardly ask him to hide it for her.

"You're upset with me, aren't you?" he asked, breaking her trance.

"No." She shook her head, getting her thoughts in order. "I think all this stuff with Maria has been getting to me. Also..."

"What?"

She flashed a sheepish smile. "I'm hungry."

"Subtlety isn't really your thing, is it?" He rolled his eyes as he backed up. "I'll grab food and be right back."

"Thank you," she called after him.

Over dinner, Lily told Flynn about her conversation with Maria. Chatting it through felt cathartic, and she wished she could talk to him about the issue with her backpack.

But while it might make her feel better to confide in him, it would cause a lot of stress for Flynn. It wasn't fair to put that on him.

Lying in bed after he'd left, her mind wouldn't settle. She didn't even know for definite that she was looking for the thief in the right place. Maybe she was barking up the wrong tree altogether.

The artists had been nearby for at least two of the thefts, though. Plus, there was the pencil she'd found. There was also the small point that she had no other leads.

Sadly, she was out of excuses for going back to visit the art retreat. Unless she wanted to spend thousands of pounds on a painting she didn't even like.

Waiting for the kettle to boil the following morning, she trawled her brain, but all she could come up with was hanging around outside and waiting until they went off on one of their trips. Who knew when that would be though.

She'd just have to go up there and try to sneak in. If she were caught, she'd come up with an excuse. The forgotten sunglasses line might have to be used again. With Jessica not due to come into work until lunchtime, and a delivery of fresh fruit and herbs due to be delivered from the garden centre, she was tied to the shop for the morning, anyway.

It would have to be an afternoon trip for the sleuthing.

With no one around when she reached Gideon's place, Lily couldn't tell if the group was on an excursion or if they were just hidden away in their rooms. She walked confidently past the big house, trying to look like someone who was supposed to be there.

The front door of the guest accommodation was unlocked. Had they really all gone out without locking the door? Maybe they were just in a nearby field or somewhere close enough that they hadn't felt the need to lock up.

Whatever the reason, Lily fully intended to take advantage of their negligence. Except, the lack of resistance when she tried Roland's door made her wonder if it was all a little too easy. Somehow, she felt as though she was walking into a trap. There was no way she was stopping, though. She had her chance to search his room, and she was taking it.

Quietly, she closed the door behind her, then flinched at a sound from inside the room.

Snoring.

She almost didn't dare look.

Slowly, she turned and squinted – as though she had less chance of being spotted if she closed her eyes.

Roland was lying on the bed, fully dressed but fast asleep. That explained the unlocked doors, then.

As curse words rang out in Lily's mind, she reached for the door again, but hesitated as her fingers landed on the cool handle.

He was snoring at a regular rhythm, so he was probably in a deep sleep. Could she search the room while he was right there in it?

All she needed was a few minutes. There really wasn't any way to explain it if she got caught, but at this point she was desperate enough to take that chance.

The least she could do was a quick scan from where she was standing. When that showed nothing unusual, she moved to the wardrobe, gritting her teeth as she opened the door, hoping the hinges would make no sound. It was empty apart from a few items of clothing. She didn't close the door fully, deciding it wasn't worth the chance of it making a noise.

As she cautiously opened the three drawers in the dresser, she was fairly sure the sound of her heart beat should wake Roland, but the purr of his snores continued.

Next, she stuck her head into the bathroom, but there was nothing in there.

She was running out of places to look.

Crouching at the end of the bed, she peered underneath but only found the bare floorboards.

The snoring stopped abruptly, and she was fairly sure her heart stopped at the same time.

Another slew of swear words rampaged through her head.

And then the snoring started up again, and she released a slow, quiet breath.

She'd pushed her luck far enough for one day. Thankfully, the door opened quietly, and she breathed a sigh of relief when she was out in the hallway.

The silence was broken by the sound of someone clearing their throat.

Saffron stood in the kitchen doorway, hands on her hips as she stared at Lily.

Chapter Fifteen

Lily suspected the line about looking for her sunglasses wouldn't cut it today. With Saffron glaring at her from the end of the hall, she stayed completely still, considering her move.

"Caught you," Saffron whispered with a mischievous glint in her eyes.

"This isn't what it looks like," Lily replied frantically.

"Don't worry." Her eyes softened. "Your secret is safe with me. I promise I won't tell anyone."

Lily frowned, dazed.

"He's old for you though, isn't he?" Saffron remarked, her eyes shifting to Roland's door.

Blinking rapidly, Lily walked along the hall. "Excuse me?"

"I mean, you're both adults, so I say do what you want – I just wouldn't have guessed it."

"No!" Lily said, not stopping to think about the fact that she was about to blow her own cover. "That's really not what was going on."

"I promise I can be discreet," Saffron said. "Us girls have to stick together. If anyone asks, I'll say you're here visiting me. Okay?"

"Umm... that would actually be great. Thank you."

A door along the hall opened, and Martha walked out of her room. "Hello again," she said shyly.

"Lily's here to visit me," Saffron announced. "We got on so well the other day. Some people just have an instant connection, don't they? That's what happened with us. I bet we'll be friends for life. Don't you think, Lily?"

Probably not. Lily nodded weakly.

"Would you like a cuppa?" Martha asked.

"I don't want to put you to any trouble..."

"I'd like it if you stayed for a drink," Martha replied. "I feel terrible about yesterday, and I hope you'll let me apologise."

With no idea what she was talking about, Lily waited, hoping she'd explain herself.

"It was nothing to do with you. I'm not even convinced I fully registered you were there. The phone call was intense, and I was focused on that. I realised afterwards how rude I'd been."

"It's fine," Lily said. "I didn't think much about it. I interrupted you, so it was probably my fault."

"That's kind of you to say."

"Was it your husband on the phone?" Saffron asked. "Is everything okay? I'll bet he's missing you."

"I think he is." Martha moved to stare out of the window, apparently forgetting about making drinks. "I'll be back home in a few days, and it'll only be ten days altogether. You'd think he'd manage on his own for ten days, but he's clingy."

"That would drive me crazy," Saffron said. "I'm such a free spirit – I could never put up with someone making demands of me. I bet you're the same, Lily. Are you strictly a 'no strings' kind of person too?"

"I'm not sure I'd say that," Lily mumbled, her stomach turning at the conclusion Saffron had reached about her and Roland. "How long have you been married?" she asked Martha.

"Far too long," she muttered, then sighed heavily. "Twenty-six years."

"Aren't you missing him at all?" Saffron asked.

"You'll think I'm awful, but no. I'm having a wonderful time, and it's only marred by his nightly phone calls."

"How sad," Saffron mused. "Have you ever thought of leaving him?"

"I think about it all the time, but I can't imagine actually doing it." She looked lost in thought for a moment. "Although while I've been here, I have wondered if maybe it's possible..."

"Anything is possible," Saffron said eagerly. "I can help you make a plan for a new life if you'd like. I'm great at that kind of thing. It'd give me a thrill to help you come up with ideas for your new life."

Martha seemed to ponder the idea. "I don't know. It feels wrong even considering it." She shook her head and left the room.

Lily stared after her, wondering what it was about her time at the retreat that made her feel as though leaving her husband was a possibility. Stealing a backpack full of cash, perhaps? That would probably make someone feel they had more options in life.

"I have to get back to work," Lily told Saffron.

"Thank you for coming to visit me," Saffron said with a cheeky wink.

Out of ideas for where to look next, Lily wandered slowly outside. Aside from Gideon's private rooms, she'd searched everywhere she could think of. Though maybe the thief had been more creative about where they stashed their goods.

"Can't keep away, can you?" Gideon's voice drew her attention to the studio, where he was standing in the doorway.

"I struck up a friendship with Saffron," she replied. "Just called in to say hello."

"She's cheerful. I'll give her that. Enthusiastic is the only good thing I can say about her artistic abilities, but I should be used to that by now." He puffed out a breath. "When I opened this place as a retreat, I naïvely thought I'd be mingling with like-minded souls, and others with artistic talent such as my own. Sadly, all I get are washed up housewives trying to fill a gap in their lives, or ragtag wannabes who beg to come despite not being able to pay for accommodation." His gaze went pointedly to Silas's tent. "Not an ounce of artistic talent among the lot of them. I try not to let it get me down, but I can't say that's easy."

"It must be enjoyable too," Lily ventured. "Getting to meet all kinds of people. Plus, you get to do what you love for a living. I think that's what most people dream of."

"I suppose I shouldn't grumble." Bending, he picked something from the floor.

Wrapped in his fist, Lily almost missed that it was an identical pencil to the one she'd found at her place.

"Marketing materials?" she asked, tipping her head at it.

"Yes. The guests expect some sort of goodie bag. So they told me in the reviews. That's what other places do. Or so they say." He rolled the pencil between his thumb and forefinger. "So now I give out a little welcome pack."

"They're just for guests, then?"

"Oh, you're welcome to as many as you like." Misunderstanding the question, he moved inside and reappeared with a handful of them. "Bane of my existence, these things. As though I don't have enough junk to contend with, I went and added an extra zero to the order by mistake. Now they seem to be everywhere I look. I give them away to everyone I meet, but the stash doesn't seem to decrease."

Lily's heart sank. All the time she'd spent assuming the thief was someone from the retreat and it could have been anyone.

"I'll just take a couple," she said, handing the rest of the pencils back. "Thank you."

"You're welcome." He told her to have a good day, and she left feeling utterly disheartened. Maybe she'd never see her backpack again.

The only good thing was that the police didn't seem to be having any more luck than her. So long as they didn't find her stuff, she was okay.

Chapter Sixteen

A FEMININE VOICE pulled Lily from her thoughts as she ambled down the lane away from Gideon's place.

"Excuse me!" the woman in front of the cottage called, waving madly.

"Hi," Lily said, glancing around to check she wasn't actually trying to get the attention of someone else.

"It's Lily, isn't it?"

"Yes." With a nervous smile, she veered in her direction.

"I don't mean to bother you, but I've seen you walking past several times."

"Oh." Her smile wavered. "I like to stretch my legs and make sure I get my steps in for the day."

"I wondered if you were investigating?"

Lily fixed her features into a confused expression.

"I've heard you do that sort of thing," the well-dressed woman said quickly. "And I was actually hoping you were. I don't feel safe in my home any more. And I wanted to let you know that if you wanted to speak to me about the burglary, I'd be very happy to tell you everything I know. I've already told the police everything, and I don't think I was at all helpful, but just in case you had questions, I'd be very willing to speak with you."

Realisation dawned on Lily. "You were burgled?"

"Yes. I want the culprit found, and I don't care who finds them."

Lily felt a little stupid. She'd been so sure she knew who the suspects were that she hadn't even thought of speaking to anyone who'd been robbed. Maybe questioning the woman would be helpful.

"Would you like to come in for a few minutes?" the woman asked. "I'm Hilary, by the way. Hilary Phillips."

"Nice to meet you," Lily said, walking to the front door with her.

"It's actually a relief that you're looking into this," Hilary said, closing the door behind them and gesturing to the minimalistic living room on the right. "I know the police do their best, but they're always stretched. And, as I said to my husband, it'll be easier for you to look into things when you're not bound to rules and procedure. Also, people will be guarded around police officers, won't they?"

"I think the police do a great job," Lily said, feeling slightly uncomfortable at the conversation.

"They do! Don't get me wrong – I didn't mean to say anything against them. Only that I'm glad you're looking into it too. I'm absolutely beside myself thinking there's such a person out there. I don't even care about what they took. It's the fact that they were in my home." Her shoulders shook as she shuddered. "It gives me the creeps."

"I imagine it must feel awful," Lily said, knowing exactly how awful it felt. "Can you tell me everything you remember from that night?"

Hilary nodded eagerly, then launched into a waffly account that provided no more information than Lily had got from Flynn. "It's probably not helpful," she said eventually.

Lily smiled. It really *wasn't* helpful, but she didn't like to say that she'd hit a dead end.

"I'm going to keep looking into it."

"Thank you. I'm so grateful."

"If I could ask you a small favour," Lily said, standing. "I'd appreciate it if you didn't mention to anyone that I'm investigating this."

"Definitely." Hilary's eyes widened. "I totally understand. It would be much harder to look into people if they knew you were after them."

"Yes." That hadn't been entirely what she was thinking. "It's probably also best if you don't let the police know that you spoke to me. I always keep them informed of anything I find, but until I find something, I prefer to keep things quiet."

"I imagine they might feel you're undermining their profession or something." She dragged an imaginary zip across her lips. "Mum's the word. Just let me know if I can help."

"Thank you." Back in the hallway, Lily's gaze snagged on an envelope on the console table. "Is that for Len Marrack?" she asked, tipping her head at the envelope with *Len* scribbled across it.

"Yes. Lovely man. We always pay him in cash. He prefers that. Heart of gold he has. Sweeps out the gutters for us at no extra cost. If there were more Len Marracks, the world would be a better place."

Lily mumbled her agreement, but her mind was whirring with a brand-new theory as she stepped out of the house.

After checking the Mermaid Inn to see if Seren was working – and finding she wasn't – Lily realised she had her very own source of local knowledge right in her ice cream shop. Jessica could probably tell her where Len lived.

Focused on getting back to the shop, she almost didn't spot Len rushing out of Pippa's cafe. Even if she hadn't looked up in time, his booming voice would have got her attention as he ranted into his phone.

He stopped on the other side of the promenade, staring out to sea as he continued his conversation.

"It's got to be tomorrow," he bellowed. "We already agreed on it."

Lily inched closer, hoping he wouldn't spot her hovering behind him.

"You'll get your usual cut," he retorted. "If I give you more, it's not worth it for me. All you have to do is load it onto the Scillonian, then hand it over to my guy at the other end. It's pretty much no work for you."

He shook his head and let out a low grumble. "I know things are hectic at the harbour, but things are always hectic. This can't wait. I'll see you in the morning." It seemed he'd cut off the call to avoid giving the person on the other end a chance to argue.

"Afternoon, Len!" Lily said cheerfully.

"Hello, Lily," he said, but barely looked at her as he took off, striding along the promenade towards the pub.

He'd always seemed like a salt of the earth kind of guy, but wouldn't that perception make it all the easier for him to get away with committing crimes? Plus, given his profession, he'd know exactly who left the doors unlocked and when the best times to rob people were. He'd even be able to peer into their windows beforehand and check what he wanted to grab. Anyone seeing him would assume he was working.

Being a window cleaner was the perfect alibi for theft. Especially for someone like Len, who people trusted.

It was sad to think he'd break that trust, but Lily couldn't afford to dwell on that.

For now, all she had to focus on was finding her backpack.

Chapter Seventeen

With the shop busier than it had been for a while, Lily waited until they'd closed before setting off to Len's house. She didn't have much of a plan. Other than crossing her fingers he was out and had conveniently left his door open and a bunch of stolen goods lying out.

That seemed overly optimistic.

Not that she needed him to have left all the stolen goods lying out. Just her backpack would do. That was all she really needed. She'd let this case go if she could just get her hands on that passport.

Maybe she would anyway. She couldn't swear to that.

It was almost seven when she walked onto Church Street. The smell of barbecue coals wafted, making her mouth water. She'd have to drop some hints for a barbecue dinner the next time she saw Seren or Kit.

Standing outside Len's house, she looked through the open garage door to the small garden at the back where the smoke was wafting from.

"The next guest is here," a wobbly guy who Lily vaguely recognised as a regular at the Mermaid Inn called across the garden.

Len stepped into view, wearing a blue and white striped apron and holding a pair of tongs in his hand.

"Oh, no! I've been caught out. Someone else I forgot to invite." He handed the tongs to the inebriated guy and set off towards Lily. "How are you?"

"Fine, thank you."

"Every time I invite people over, I end up feeling guilty about the people I didn't invite. It's just a little shindig with a few friends, but you're welcome to join."

"No, it's fine. I wasn't worried about not getting an invitation."

"Some people around here would actually get annoyed with me, you know? As though I can fit everyone I know in my tiny little garden." He smiled brightly. "Anyway, what can I do for you?"

"How do you mean?"

"I assume you weren't just passing?"

"No. I… umm…" She glanced around, stalling for time and grasping for inspiration. "I've actually been a bit worried since our conversation the other day…"

"What conversation?"

"The one about Gideon not paying you enough for cleaning the windows. I wondered afterwards if that was you hinting that I don't pay you enough. Because if the price has gone up, you only need to say. I'd hate to think I was underpaying you."

He rested a hand on her arm. "That's very sweet of you, but not an issue. My problem is some longstanding customers who get shirty with me for raising my prices from time to time. Some people think they should pay me the same as they were paying me fifteen years ago, but the world doesn't work like that."

"I see," Lily said. "I just wanted to check there was no problem between us."

"Not at all." He tilted his head. "You're one of my favourite customers, you are!"

"I'll bet you say that to everyone," she joked.

Or maybe he was saying it because he was now thirty grand better off because of her.

He leaned close and whispered. "Just the ones who give me free ice cream."

The warmth in his voice made her laugh, and for a moment she forgot he was her number one suspect. She really didn't want it to be him who'd been stealing from people.

"I should let you get back to your friends," she said, tipping her chin. "That smells delicious, by the way. It's making my stomach rumble."

He tipped his head back as he laughed. "I can't send you away now, can I?"

"I wasn't hinting..." She had been, actually. And hadn't even tried to be subtle.

As he led her through the garage, she checked her watch. In half an hour she was supposed to be at Flynn's place for dinner. She could probably scout the place out quickly and still make it over there. Otherwise, she'd just tell him she'd be late.

It took twenty minutes of small talk with the group of older men before Lily found a break in the chatter to ask to use the bathroom.

Len directed her upstairs without hesitation. She didn't bother listening to the rest of the directions since she planned on having a good snoop around, anyway.

With the chatter from the garden letting her know she was safe to search, she got straight to work. After rummaging through every cupboard and drawer in his bedroom, she went to the small box room and did the same there.

Nothing unusual to be found. Like Gideon's place, there was a lot of clutter and what seemed to be an excess of vacuum cleaners. A few moving boxes were flattened and leaning against the wall in the box room, so she assumed he hadn't lived there too long.

Frustrated by her fruitless search, she made a quick stop at the bathroom and ventured back downstairs.

"Lovely little house," she said to Len.

He rolled his eyes. "That's very polite of you. It's a pokey house, which is a complete mess, but I appreciate your tact. Can I tempt you with another burger?"

"I'd love one, but I'm actually supposed to meet Flynn."

"PC Grainger?" He grinned. "He's a good guy. Shame he's leaving."

"Yeah." Lily was about to make a break for it before realising she was missing an opportunity. Anyone with stolen goods in their house probably wouldn't be keen to have a police officer around. Even an off-duty one.

"Would you mind if I tell him to meet me here instead?" she asked innocently. "I don't want to cancel on him, but I'm not sure I can bring myself to pass up another of your burgers. They're the best I've tasted in a long time."

"The more the merrier," he said without missing a beat. "This lot might behave better with a copper around the place too."

"Don't count on it," one of them called. "PC Grainger's in the pub all the time and none of us behave there."

Suddenly, inviting Flynn felt like a bad idea. She'd only wanted to see how Len would react. His lack of reaction made her question whether she might yet again be on entirely the wrong track.

Chapter Eighteen

The message from Lily was odd. Flynn contemplated calling to ask why exactly she was inviting him to a party at the local window cleaner's house, then decided not to bother. There'd be some convoluted reason, he was sure. Better just to go along with it.

He arrived at the address she sent and was subjected to some good-natured banter about the arrival of the police officer at the party.

It was almost an hour before he got Lily alone. Wedged together on a small bench at the corner of the garden, he took a swig of his beer and spoke quietly.

"Why exactly are we at a party with a bunch of old men?"

"Long story," she whispered. "But essentially because Len cleans my windows, and it felt rude to decline the invitation."

"Keep talking," he said, amused. "That's definitely not the real reason. I know you, remember?"

She made some attempt at looking innocent, then huffed in defeat. "Fine. I thought maybe Len was the person committing the thefts."

"Len Marrack? The window cleaner?"

"Yes. Think about it. He knows everyone's routines and

everyone's security measures. Or lack of security measures. People trust him."

"That's all you're basing your theory on?"

"No. I heard him on the phone talking about transporting goods to the mainland. He sounded agitated. Also, he cleans Hilary Phillips's windows."

"How on earth did you come by that information?" A trickle of discomfort stirred in his stomach. Not that he was surprised at her looking into the thefts. Usually, she wasn't secretive about her investigations, though. "Have you been looking into this?"

"Not exactly. Hilary came to me and asked if I was investigating. I think she assumed I would be. So she gave me her account of the burglary, and it came up that Len Marrack cleans their windows."

"That just came into the conversation?"

"Why are you nitpicking? Do you want a blow-by-blow account of the conversation with everything word for word?"

He rolled his eyes, happy that she at least seemed to have her usual spark back. "So you got suspicious about Len and came over here to suss him out?"

"Yes."

"I suppose I'm supposed to say I need the loo, then rummage around for evidence."

"No. The toilet's upstairs, and I already looked there. You need to check the downstairs."

He laughed lightly. "I can't do that. Also, your theory is pretty flimsy. The fact that people trust him might make it easy for him to commit crimes, but don't you think it also means he's the type of person who wouldn't rob people blind? He's been working for these people for years. Why would he suddenly start stealing from them?"

"I don't know." She gave a dramatic shrug. "He was complaining about some people not properly compensating him for his work and expecting him to work for cheap. Also, he's getting on a bit. He mentioned having arthritis in his hands.

Maybe he's thinking of retirement and now seems like the perfect time to top up his pension."

"I can't snoop around his house."

"You don't really need to. Just think of an excuse and ask if you can go inside. I want to see how he reacts to having a police officer in his home."

He really should have argued, but he hardly hesitated at all before heading for the patio table and scooping up salsa with a tortilla chip. Tilting his hand at the last minute sent salsa dripping down his hand.

"Got any napkins, Len?" he said, shoving the tortilla in his mouth and raising his sticky palm to their host. "Don't get up. Just point me in the right direction."

"I'm not that posh," Len called over the noise of his friends chatting loudly. "I doubt you'll find napkins, but there'll be kitchen roll. Kitchen's at the front."

He wandered inside, thinking that Len didn't seem like someone who had something to hide.

In the kitchen he washed his hands, then dried them on his jeans and stood looking around the messy kitchen. He wasn't doing anything wrong, so his reaction to Lily creeping up behind him and digging her fingers in either side of his waist was slightly dramatic.

"Why are you so jumpy?" she asked as he turned. "Up to no good?"

"You get me into some really dubious situations, you know?"

"Yeah, but I keep life interesting."

"Can't argue with that," he said, circling his arms around her and pulling her close.

Forgetting the search, he kissed her eagerly. "Can we leave soon?" he asked.

"Yeah." Her eyes darted around the room. "If Len's hiding something, he clearly isn't concerned about us finding it. So it's not in a place we'd just stumble over it."

"I think you're wrong about Len," he whispered. "He seems

like a decent guy. And it definitely doesn't appear he has anything to hide."

"Or he's hidden it well."

"Let's just go home," he said.

He kissed her again, and that was all the convincing she needed.

"Yes," she agreed. "Let's go."

Sadly, it wasn't that easy to get away. Len insisted they stay and drink shots, which Flynn wriggled out of due to being on call, but Lily had no such excuse and got swept up in knocking back ouzo with the group of men. They got dragged into card games after that, and since it was all actually pretty entertaining, they ended up staying for another hour.

Finally, it was Len who got everyone moving.

"Kicking out time, I'm afraid," he said at half ten. "It's past my bedtime. Us old people can't stay up into the early hours. Off you go, the lot of you."

He waved away offers to help tidy up, and Flynn was amused by Lily's alcohol-fuelled smile by the time the two of them ambled away down the road.

"Do you want to stay at my place?" he asked hopefully.

"I prefer my place," she said, bumping against him.

"I don't have my uniform at your place," he pointed out. "So either we need to go to mine and get it, then go to yours. Or we just go to mine."

"I get the impression you're hinting it will be easier just to go to yours."

"My bed is also comfier than yours."

"True," she agreed. "But your place doesn't have ice cream."

"Funnily enough, it's not something I keep in stock these days."

"Strange, that. Are you on some kind of health kick?"

He tugged on her hand, drawing her closer. "Are you drunk?"

"Tipsy," she said.

"Let's swing by the pub."

She frowned. "I don't want to drink any more."

"Not to drink. I just want to check it's all quiet down there. With Sergeant Proctor under the weather, and PC Hill away, there'll be no one doing the usual patrol down there. I don't want to get settled at home and then get called out to a bar brawl." This time when he got Lily alone, he didn't want any interruptions.

"How many bar brawls have you seen while you've been here?"

"I believe there've been two calls to the pub, but PC Hill went to deal with it both times and it was all sorted by the time he arrived on the scene."

"Not very likely then."

"When I absolutely don't want to get a call, you can guarantee that'll be the time I do. Like the other night."

"Pub it is then, if you insist."

"Just to clarify, you're not drinking any more alcohol."

"Really? Since when are you the boss of me?"

"Since I don't want you passing out on me when I get you home."

A smile curled her lips. "Fair call. I won't drink any more."

Instead, they sat at the bar with glasses of water, chatting with Seren and Noah while they cleaned up the pub.

Once Flynn was satisfied there wouldn't be any trouble, they wandered back outside, and he followed Lily's lead when she turned the corner to the harbour. When she stopped to watch the moonlight dance on the gentle waves, he slipped his arms around her waist, and she leaned contentedly with her back propped against his chest.

A surge of sentimentality hit him. "I'm going to miss the quiet," he said against her hair. "It's so peaceful here."

She let out a hum of acknowledgement, but said nothing.

"I was thinking about what we'll do when I'm back in

London," he said, eyes fixed on the hypnotic twinkle of moonlight on waves.

She tensed in his arms. "Don't talk about that now."

"We should make a plan, though, for when we'll see each other next. I'll need some time to settle back into my routines, so I thought you could visit me first..."

"Flynn," she sighed. "You're ruining the moment."

"I just think it'll be easier if we have a solid plan."

"Maybe. But let's talk about it nearer the time."

"There isn't that much time..." His words trailed off when she turned and kissed him.

"Let's go home," she said, taking his hand and leading the way.

He bit his tongue to stop himself from pushing the conversation. Obviously, now wasn't the time to discuss it.

It was after midnight when he closed the door to his flat behind them and caught her mouth in a kiss that was needy and insistent.

They made it to the bedroom without their lips parting, but she broke the intensity of the moment by giggling as soon as he had her on her back.

"I'm not sure what you find funny," he said, smiling down at her. "This is a serious moment."

"I know, but I keep thinking your phone is going to ring."

"The entire island is asleep in bed. No one is out getting up to no good now. Which means we're safe to get up to no good in my bed."

"Okay then. Carry on."

He didn't even kiss her again before his phone erupted with its obnoxiously loud ringtone.

"What did you do?" he complained, jumping off her.

She laughed. "What do you mean, *what did I do?*"

"You jinxed it! Why did you have to mention the phone?"

"I'm not sure you have any grounds to blame me here."

He glared at her before swiping a finger over his phone screen. "PC Flynn Grainger," he stated in his police officer voice.

Chapter Nineteen

Lily flopped back on Flynn's pillows and listened to him on the phone, fairly certain the call was about to send him running out of the door.

When he ended the call and didn't immediately move, she had a spark of hope that she'd misread the conversation.

"That was the control room," he said, pulling his T-shirt over his head. "They tried to get hold of the sergeant, but he's not answering the phone."

"Was there another break in?"

"No." When he removed his jeans, she thought he wasn't going anywhere. Until she realised he was changing into his uniform. "There have been a couple of phone calls from people who think they've seen someone lurking. One of them wasn't even sure, but their dogs were barking, and they got worried because of recent events. It could just be people being jumpy, but I need to check."

She sat up and watched him button up his shirt. "Can I come?"

"Not really." He flashed an apologetic look. "If anyone finds out I let you do a ride along, I'll be in trouble."

"You're going in the car?"

"Yeah. Why?"

"That's a bad plan. We should run."

He stopped and stared at her. "Excuse me?"

"It'll be quicker." She wrinkled her nose. "Well, not quicker since we're not actually that fast, but we're fit."

"What are you talking about?"

"If the thief is out there, they'll see the police car coming. It'll scare them off. If we go on foot, we have the element of surprise. Tell me that doesn't make sense."

"It sort of makes sense," he said begrudgingly.

"This isn't London," she said. "Things are different here." She bounded off the bed. "Let's go catch a bad guy."

"All right," he said eventually. "I'll just have to tell control they'll need to reach me on my mobile." While he did that, he went to put his boots on, but Lily pushed them aside and put his running shoes in front of him instead.

"What are you doing now?" he asked when he got off the phone.

"If you run in those boots, you may as well turn up with the sirens blaring. They'll hear you coming from here. Plus, you'll be slow in your boots."

"I'm actually pretty used to running in my boots." He didn't argue further though, just shoved his feet into his trainers and made for the door.

The jog sobered Lily up entirely. At a remote cottage on the northern side of the island, she hung back while Flynn went to speak to the man who'd called the police. Apparently, he seemed a little sheepish – not sure now that the shadows he'd seen had really been a person at all.

His neighbours – half a mile away – reported that their usually docile dogs had been barking like crazy around half an hour ago. It was very close to the time the guy claimed to have seen someone lurking.

Half an hour had passed though, so presumably if someone had been there, they weren't around any more. The two of them wandered the dark lanes for three quarters of an hour and were talking about heading home when the dispatcher called Flynn's mobile and told him another call had just come in from Mirren Treneary – saying she'd spotted someone in her garden. He started to give the address, but Flynn told him he didn't need it and would call him back to keep him updated.

"Old Town Bay," Lily said as they shifted into a slow jog.

"I don't think we've got much hope of catching him now."

"Why not?"

"It's Mirren Treneary. What are the chances she hasn't called her sons? And then what are the chances that twenty Treneary men haven't just descended on her and scared whoever it was off?"

"There aren't twenty of them," Lily said with a smile.

"There are enough to intimidate any sane person."

"True."

They hadn't got far when Flynn's phone rang again. He looked at the screen. "It's Trystan Treneary."

"Put him on speaker," Lily said as they slowed their pace.

"I'm on my way," Flynn said when he answered. "Are you with your mum?"

"I'm at my place, but Denzel's with Mum, so she's fine. Noah and I can be there in a matter of seconds if needed, but for now we're keeping the lights off and lurking behind the curtains trying to spot whoever's out there. Kit and Seren are doing the same around the other side of the bay, and I've rung around as many neighbours as I can wake up. Everyone's sitting in the dark, keeping watch. The chatter on the WhatsApp group is pretty entertaining."

"But there's no sign of them now?" Flynn asked.

"No. Mum and Denzel are certain they heard someone. They could only make out shadows, but they're both convinced it was a person."

"Sounds as though you have everything under control, but we're on our way."

"Is the sergeant with you? Mum couldn't get hold of him, and she didn't have your number, so she called 999."

"I'm actually with Lily."

A low chuckle emanated down the phone. "Even better!" Trystan said cheerfully. "This is turning into quite a party. You're not in the car, are you?"

"No." Flynn slid a look at Lily. "I decided it would be better to come on foot and not risk scaring them off with the headlights."

"Good idea. Since there's no sign of anyone here, I'd imagine they disappeared out the other side of Mum's garden. Why not cut round the other way and see if you don't bump into them around there. If anyone here spots them, I'll let you know."

"Perfect," Flynn said. "I'll keep you updated."

Lily waited a moment after Flynn ended the call.

"What was it you were saying about the Trenearys barging in and scaring the thief away?"

"I don't even know why they need police over here. Apparently, people can fend for themselves." He flashed her a smile and increased the tempo.

Five minutes later, they slowed again, hugging the side of the lane and keeping their limited conversations to a hushed whisper.

"We should split up," Lily suggested eventually. "We can cover more ground that way."

She expected resistance, but he gave a curt nod.

"If you see anyone, call me immediately."

"I will. And I'm sure you'd hear me if I screamed."

He stepped close to her. "I've seen you make grown men whimper. I can't imagine it'll be your screams I hear. Be careful though." He kissed her hairline so casually that it felt unexpectedly intimate.

She took the lane to the left while he went right, toward Mirren's house.

All the confidence she'd felt with Flynn at her side seeped away, and her senses shifted into high alert. The smallest sound made her twitchy, and the shadows seemed more pronounced.

Telling herself Flynn was nearby, and that there was an entire fleet of Trenearys not far away either, she continued up the lane to where a few lonely cottages stood at intervals on the eastern side of the island. She slowed as she approached the first house. Peering into the garden, her heart sped up at the sound of a tree branch scratching quietly at the slate roof every time the breeze tugged at it.

Her eyes were used to the dim moonlight by now, and there was no sign of anyone around the house. The inside was quiet too, and she wondered whether Trystan had been in touch with them and if they were peeking out at her from behind their curtains. Amused by the thought, she gave a quick salute to the upstairs window and continued on her way.

At the next cottage, she slipped off the road and crept around the back. Clouds had blocked the moonlight, and it was like a dimmer switch being turned down.

Just as she was about to cut back up to the lane, she spotted something between her and the next cottage along.

Some*one,* not some*thing*.

Instinct had her rooted to the spot. It took a moment for her to figure out that the man was walking away from her, not towards her. His gait was unhurried, and he stopped completely just before he reached the next cottage. With his head bent, he appeared as though he was writing something down. At thirty metres or so from Lily, she didn't dare try to get any closer. He'd hear the slightest sound.

So she kept her eyes on him as she pulled out her phone. Quickly, she tapped out a message to Flynn.

Come my way, she told him. *I have my eye on someone. Stick to the lane. Come quietly. I'm at the second house you come to.*

His reply came immediately. *On my way.*

With bated breath, Lily watched the man straighten up and take a few steps towards the house. A security light bathed him in a yellow glow, and he raised his hand to his face.

Feeling illogically as though it had illuminated her too, Lily moved into the shadow of the house.

The man walked briskly to the lane, and she resisted the urge to chase after him. Flynn would be here in a second, and she could go with him. Reaching the lane, the man glanced in her direction, and she told herself there was no way he could see her.

She could see him, though.

His beanie was pulled down to his eyes, but the pointy chin, accentuated by a goatee beard, was very familiar.

As recognition hit her, she moved around the house and up to the lane. She'd lost sight of him, and suddenly she didn't care about waiting for Flynn. She burst into a run and tore down the road, only to reach a fork just after the bend. He could have gone one of three ways, and she couldn't see anyone in any direction. At a noise behind her, she turned and waited for Flynn.

"What did you see?" he asked, quiet but breathless.

"A man. He seemed to be sizing up that cottage down there, but the security light came on and he scarpered. I don't know which way he went."

"*He?* Did you get a good look at him?"

"Not really. It was definitely a man. He had a hat on, and I think he had a beard." She was certain it was Roland but couldn't say that since it would mean explaining how she knew Roland. That was a can of worms she'd rather keep closed. "I think he might have gone that way." She pointed along the lane, but it was merely her best guess since it was the most direct route to the art retreat.

"Let's go then," Flynn said. "We'll stick together."

Lily nodded, and they set off at a jog again.

Maybe Roland hadn't gone directly back to the retreat, or maybe he'd seen them and hidden. Maybe it hadn't been him at all. Either way, they didn't find anyone. After two hours of roaming, and no more sightings from the Trenearys or anyone else on the island, they finally gave up.

"I'm so tired," Lily said, her muscles and her mind screaming at her for rest.

Flynn nodded. "This really wasn't the physical activity I had in mind for tonight."

"I enjoyed the night anyway," she said through a yawn.

"Not as much as you'd have enjoyed all the sex I had planned."

"You're very confident, Flynn."

"Yep."

Laughing, she veered into him and stayed glued to his side as he draped an arm around her shoulders and planted a kiss on the side of her head.

Chapter Twenty

It was almost four in the morning when they finally fell into Flynn's bed. Exhausted, Lily curled into Flynn's side and was asleep within minutes. It only felt like a few more minutes before she was awake again. Flynn had already left for work, despite it only being half eight. The desire to turn over and go back to sleep was hard to ignore. Only the thought of paying Roland a visit – and retrieving her passports – got Lily moving.

She splashed water on her face and pulled her hair into a ponytail before leaving the flat. This time, she didn't need a plan to scout out the art retreat. She'd simply demand to speak to Roland alone and convince him to give up her passports. She could bribe him with the promise of keeping her money.

Not that she intended to let him get away with his crime spree – as soon as she had the forged passport safely back in her possession, she'd report him to the police. Without her passports there was nothing to connect her to the backpack. She could deny any knowledge of it.

It wasn't as though she needed the money. If she never saw it again, so be it.

. . .

"Morning!" Saffron called when Lily stepped into the guest accommodation at the art retreat.

"Hi," Lily replied, moving to join Saffron and Martha in the kitchen.

Saffron patted the seat beside her. "It's so nice of you to visit me again." The wink she gave her exuded mirth, and Lily squirmed inwardly at the thought that she really believed she was involved in a fling with Roland.

"Is Roland here?" Lily asked, deciding she didn't have time to worry about what anyone thought. She only wanted her passports back.

"You just missed him," Martha said. "He's gone for a shower."

Glancing back along the hall, Lily contemplated barging in on him in the shower. Maybe catching him off guard wouldn't be a terrible thing. She wasn't keen to see him naked, though.

"He'll be back soon," Saffron said. "He's promised to show us his sketches. There's coffee in the pot if you want some."

"Thanks." She poured herself a mug, unsure whether caffeine was a great idea given the amount of adrenaline pumping through her system.

Martha frowned when Lily sat down. "I don't mean to sound rude, but why did you want to see Roland?"

"She probably wants to see his sketches too," Saffron said, her eyes on her phone as she scrolled away. "All his secrecy around his charcoal sketches makes them very intriguing."

Lily took a sip of coffee to avoid having to answer and was grateful that Roland chose that moment to appear. His brow was furrowed even before he clapped eyes on Lily, but he looked even more unsure of himself then.

"I didn't hear you arrive," he mumbled.

Lily rose from her chair. "Could I have a word with you? In private."

"Let him show us his sketches first," Saffron said, rubbing her hands together. "Don't keep us in suspense any longer."

Roland hugged a sketchbook to his chest. "I didn't realise there'd be someone else here."

"Don't be shy," Martha said. "I'm sure they're brilliant."

He pulled out a chair. "I've never shown them to anyone. I don't know if they're any good. I just really enjoy it."

"Show us!" Saffron demanded while Lily sank back onto her chair.

"It's only a few drawings," he muttered, setting the book on the table. "It's silly, really."

As he opened the first page, Saffron and Martha leaned in to look.

"Oh, it's not silly at all," Saffron crooned. "They're really good. I knew they would be."

"They are," Martha agreed. "You have a real talent with charcoal."

"Show us some more," Saffron said, indicating he should turn the page with a flick of her hand.

"They're gorgeous," Martha breathed. "How can you capture so much depth and emotion in black and grey?"

"That *is* good," Lily said, leaning close to admire the sketch of moonlit clouds.

"Thank you." Roland turned the page again, keeping his fingers at the very edge to avoid smudging.

The next picture showed the rough outline of a cottage beside the sea.

"You definitely found your speciality," Saffron said, as he turned the page to a picture of another remote cottage.

"I found a positive side to insomnia, that's for sure."

Lily closed her eyes briefly as her mind whirred. "You do these at night?"

"Yes. I did a few sketches of the moon when I first arrived here, and I enjoyed it. Then I sketched a little house bathed in moonlight, and I got a bit obsessed."

"They are really good," Lily agreed as he continued to turn the pages of his sketchbook.

"I'd like to say it keeps me out of mischief." Roland smiled gently. "But last night I made a few dogs bark, so I probably annoyed the owners. I also found I have to be careful not to trigger security lights. If I get too close, the whole place lights up and I lose the ambiance."

Lily rubbed her forehead. Apparently, Roland had no idea what a fuss he'd caused last night.

It seemed Lily had been wrong about him.

With the feeling she'd forgotten something important, she stayed fixed in her seat for a moment.

Her heart rate increased as she remembered the conversation she'd overheard about Len Marrack transporting goods off the island. When she'd seen Roland last night, she'd put all her suspicions about Len aside, but what if she'd been on the right track with Len?

She checked her watch. The ferry was due to leave in twenty minutes.

It was more than a twenty-minute walk to the ferry.

Apparently, she was going for an impromptu morning run.

She didn't even say goodbye.

Chapter Twenty-One

SLOWING her pace as she reached Hugh Town, it occurred to Lily that she needed a plan. Len wouldn't be moving her backpack off the island. It would be the stolen jewellery he needed to get rid of. When she found him with it, what would she do then?

Breathless from her run, she struggled to think straight. She wanted to deal with everything alone until she had her passports, but maybe that wasn't realistic.

Deciding she needed the police on hand, she called Flynn as she rushed towards the harbour.

"I need you to meet me," she said after a quick greeting.

"The sergeant isn't here yet."

"Is he okay?"

"Yeah. I spoke to him. He's fine, just running late. Which is weird, but I can't really leave at the moment."

"It's a police matter," she said.

"What's going on?"

"It's about the conversation I overheard – Len Marrack saying he was moving goods to the mainland."

"You don't seriously think it's Len, do you?"

"Yes. I think he's planning on moving his stolen goods off the island this morning via the ferry, and I need you here to arrest him when I expose him." Once Flynn carted him off, Lily could go and search his place for her backpack.

"It doesn't make sense," Flynn said. "He'll know we're making extra checks at the ferry."

"But you're checking anyone who looks suspicious. No one is going to suspect Len. Plus, he's working with a guy at the ferry. Can you please just come down here?"

"Yeah." He sounded hesitant. "Okay."

Lily told him she'd see him soon and hung up. The harbour was already busy with people boarding the ferry. Moving closer to the ship, her eyes scanned the crowd, but she couldn't pick Len out.

There was still no sign of him when Flynn appeared beside her five minutes later.

"I don't know if I've missed him," she said.

"You haven't." Flynn looked back the way he'd come. "He's here now."

"And there's his box of stolen goods," Lily said, eyes on the large cardboard box he was wheeling along on a sack barrow.

Flynn frowned. "Len's a nice guy, and he has a good reputation."

"I know. We talked about this yesterday. It's a brilliant cover. No one would suspect him. But he also knows people's schedules, and he knows who leaves their doors unlocked. No one would ever think it suspicious if he was hanging around people's property."

"Did you definitely overhear him talking about shifting stolen goods off the island?" Flynn asked sceptically.

Lily thought back. "He was saying he needed to shift stuff off the island and that he had a buyer at the other end. He sounded stressed, and he mentioned giving the guy he was talking to his *usual cut*."

"I can't just accuse him of being a thief," Flynn said.

"You don't need to," Lily muttered as Len got near. "I'll do it." She stepped into Len's path.

"Morning!" Len called, then glanced overhead. "Hopefully, the sun comes out for you later. It's not exactly ice cream weather now with all these grey clouds."

Ignoring his jovial chatter, Lily's eyes went to the box. "What have you got there?"

A frown wrinkled his brow, and he hesitated before answering. "Just some old junk I'm getting rid of."

"What do you mean, you're getting rid of it?"

"Selling it to a fella on the mainland. Why?"

Before Lily could answer, a guy in a hi-vis jacket wandered from the boat. "That's for me, I assume, Len?"

"It is indeed. Usual drill, Jason. Someone will be waiting for it at the other end."

"Wait," Lily said, when the tall, blonde ship worker – Jason, apparently – went to take the box. "Extra checks are being carried out because of the burglaries. We need to have a look in the box."

"It's an old vacuum cleaner," Len said. "Surely I'm not suspected of being a thief?"

"We're just being vigilant," Flynn said. "It's nothing personal."

"Bloody hell." Len's eyes flashed with annoyance. "I spent ages packing it up securely."

"I can vouch for Len," Jason said.

"I'm sorry," Lily said, "but you have to admit it's quite a coincidence that you suddenly need to sell your vacuum cleaner to someone on the mainland, right when there's a spate of thefts on the island."

"I wouldn't call it a coincidence at all," Len said. "And it's not my vac."

"What do you mean?" Lily demanded.

"I'm selling it for Mr and Mrs Jenkins."

"Len often sells items for other people," Jason said. "Mostly the oldies who can't cope with the internet, or people who can't be bothered with the hassle of finding a buyer. It's his own little eBay business. He's been doing it for years. It's actually a handy service he provides."

"I can show you the listing," Len said, producing his phone and tapping away. He held it out to Flynn with the listing for the vacuum cleaner.

When Flynn glanced at Lily, she looked back at him in a panic. Had she really got this completely wrong? It made total sense that it was Len. He had the means to enter people's homes undetected and...

Panic gripped her chest. Had she been so desperate to get her stuff back that she was blindly latching on to any lead she had?

"I'll have a quick look anyway," Flynn said to Len, already pulling off the tape covering the flaps of the box. "It won't take long."

"As long as you intend on packing it back together again afterwards. And be careful. If it gets damaged, they'll demand a refund."

After pulling away a bunch of packaging material, Flynn drew the vacuum cleaner from the box. The exact one from the listing on Len's phone.

"You could hide anything in a vacuum cleaner," Lily said frantically. Stolen jewellery would be easy to stash inside a vacuum cleaner. Except as she pressed the button, and the flap popped open, all she found was the vacuum bag and a puff of dust. Her heart plummeted while an uncomfortable silence hung in the air.

"Did you really think I'd been robbing people?" Len said. "My own friends and neighbours?"

"No," Lily said weakly. It seemed absurd now. "I just..."

"I reckon your investigative instincts are a bit off in this case," Jason said, helping Flynn to pack the vac away again.

"We have to check," Flynn said. "I already told you it was nothing personal."

"Sorry," Lily muttered. "I don't know what I was thinking."

Len shook his head. "If that's what you think of me, it'd probably be better if you found someone else to clean your windows in the future."

"I'm sorry," Lily said again. "I really want to find the thief, and I have to follow every lead."

Len's features softened. "I want them found too, but you can't go harassing innocent people."

"I know." Muttering a last apology, she wandered away, slowly enough that Flynn caught up with her quickly.

"What was that all about?" he asked, with a frustrated bite to his words.

"I told you, I overheard him talking... I got the wrong end of the stick."

"Why are you even looking into this?"

"I'm not, but I overheard him talking, and it felt suddenly obvious that it was him. It all added up. Except, obviously it didn't."

"You just said you want to find the thief."

"So?"

"Why are you involving yourself?"

"Because I enjoy investigating. Haven't you noticed that by now?"

"But previously there was always a reason for you to get involved. It affected you." He paused before continuing. "Do you actually see yourself as an investigator? I don't care, but I guess it always felt a little accidental before."

"It's accidental now... I thought I'd stumbled on the perpetrator. But also, it *does* affect me. St Mary's is my home. Someone robbing my neighbours doesn't sit well with me."

"Okay," he said with a sigh. "Are you going to keep looking into it?"

"I don't know."

"Just keep me updated, okay."

"Yeah. What's going on with Sergeant Proctor? Did he turn up for work?"

"He arrived right when I got off the phone with you. Apparently he overslept."

"Weird," Lily said.

"Yeah. I should get back to the station."

"I need to open the shop," Lily said, despair seeping through her.

What she really needed was a new plan for finding her backpack, and quick.

Chapter Twenty-Two

In need of a little normalcy, Lily spent the morning focusing on the simple yet satisfying task of handing out ice creams. Frustrated that she'd hit a dead end with her investigating, she reminded herself that this was how it always went – she kept asking questions and exploring possible suspects until she landed on the right person. She needed to put the feeling of defeat aside and stick with it. Eventually, she'd uncover the thief and find her backpack.

In the middle of the afternoon, she was contemplating returning to the art retreat when she spotted Saffron and Martha walking along Porthcressa Beach. Her gaze followed them until they stopped and laid out blankets on the sand. It seemed they were settling in for a while.

Lily waited ten minutes before wandering down to their spot.

"Hello!" she called when she got close, though it was only Saffron there now.

Saffron raised a hand to shield her eyes as she looked up. "We've got a few hours to spare, so we thought we'd hit the beach. Martha's here too – she's gone for a swim."

"It's a bit chilly for it," Lily said.

"I said the same, but she thinks this might be the best weather we get before we leave." She shuffled over on her blanket and gestured for Lily to sit down. "What happened to you this morning? You ran away without saying goodbye. We were all a bit confused."

"Sorry. I remembered I'd left a batch of ice cream out on the counter. I thought maybe I could salvage it."

"Any luck?"

"No." She ran her fingers through the sand. "I can't believe I did that. Such a waste."

"It could've been worse," Saffron said, then reached for the striped tote bag when a phone rang. "That's Martha's phone," she said, reaching into the bag. "It's her husband calling. She always panics about missing his calls. Do you think I should answer it?"

She didn't give Lily a chance to respond, but pressed to accept the call.

"Hello," she said brightly. "This is Saffron. Martha is swimming, but she'll be right back." A silence. "I'm another guest at the art retreat." She rolled her eyes at Lily. "The art retreat," she said louder, as though he might be hearing impaired. "Yes. The one on the Isles of Scilly." Moving the phone from her ear, she frowned at it. "I think he hung up. Didn't sound at all friendly. It makes me really sad that Martha has such a terrible relationship."

"What are you doing with my phone?" Martha asked, water dripping from her as she approached in her swimsuit.

"Your husband called, and I know you panic about missing his calls, so I answered it."

"You answered my phone?" Martha paled as she wrapped a towel around herself.

"I thought I could say hello and keep him on the phone until you got back, but he didn't sound very happy."

"What did you say?" Martha said, with a hand covering half of her face.

"Just that I was also on the art retreat. He got weird after that."

Lily hooked her arms around her bent knees, thinking back to Martha's call when she claimed not to be able to get the video to work. "He doesn't know where you are, does he?" she asked.

Shaking her head, Martha lowered herself onto the sand. "He wouldn't approve. I told him I'm visiting my sister. I made up a bunch of lies about how she was ill and needed some help for a week or two. He wasn't even happy about that, but he could hardly say no. Not when I told him Janet had offered to pay for my train fare and that she'd pay for all my food and everything. He's a bit of a stickler about money, you see."

Lily nodded. She got the picture pretty clearly.

"What am I going to say to him now?" Martha closed her eyes briefly. "I'll have to come clean."

"I'm sorry," Saffron said. "I had no idea. Have I made things really bad for you? Is he a violent man?"

"No. He'd never physically hurt me. It's the emotional and mental stuff. He's very controlling."

"Can't you leave him?" Saffron asked, toying with the beads on her chunky necklace. "He sounds awful."

"He controls the money. That's why I never felt I could leave. I can't access the bank accounts."

"How did you pay for the retreat?" Saffron asked, shock clear in her voice.

"I've been saving for years. He gives me cash for the shopping and other stuff. So I saved the change. Just little bits here and there, but it all adds up. I opened a secret bank account using my sister's address and have been squirrelling money away. I didn't even know what I was saving it for. In the back of my mind, I thought maybe I'd be brave enough to leave him one day."

She paused, her bottom lip quivering. "When I retired, I suggested a holiday might be nice, but he didn't like the idea. So I decided to do something just for me. I used my savings, and I lied to Gregory about where I was going."

"How awful," Saffron muttered.

"I've had a lovely time," Martha said. "And I keep thinking, maybe I don't need to go back to him." Her eyes brightened as she looked up at Saffron. "You've inspired me with all your stories of your adventures. You make me think I could have adventures too. Maybe I won't be sailing off into the sunset like you," she said, eyes flashing with amusement. "But I could do something with my life."

"You could do anything you want," Saffron said, then rooted in her wicker bag for a pair of oversized sunglasses.

"Did Saffron tell you about her next adventure?" Martha asked Lily.

Lily gave a confused shrug. "No."

"I totally forgot!" Saffron said. "I'm going on a sailing trip."

"Really?" Lily asked, not fully concentrating as she pondered Martha's situation. She didn't seem like a thief, but desperate times could push people to act out of character. And it really sounded as though she was desperate.

If she were the one who stole Lily's money, she wouldn't even begrudge her that. In fact, she'd be okay with Martha having it if it meant she could get away from her husband. She just needed to give the passports back.

Lily tuned back into the conversation as Saffron beamed beside her. "I posted on some local community boards," she was saying. "Asking for a job on the island, because I thought I'd like to stay a little longer. I asked for something with accommodation included and said I was happy to do any kind of work. You won't believe my luck!" She clapped her hands together. "I got offered a job as a nanny on a yacht!"

Lily made an appropriate noise of excitement.

"I have to leave with them tomorrow. That's the only downside – cutting the art retreat short, but only by a couple of days, and I think it will be worth it. The family's regular nanny had to fly home due to a death in the family, so they needed someone to step in, and they saw my advert. It's so great. I get a nice room on the yacht and a free sailing trip. The pay is pretty good. And the kids seem very polite and well behaved. I went and met them all this morning and looked around the yacht. I'm so excited. It's really unbelievable how these things just fall into my lap. The universe is always looking out for me, that much is certain."

"It seems like it," Lily said. "The trip sounds fantastic. So you're leaving tomorrow?"

"Yes." She pouted. "I would have come to say goodbye to you. No way I'd have left without seeing you. Let's swap numbers so we can stay in touch."

"Okay." Lily pulled her phone out and forced herself to focus as they exchanged numbers.

As she walked back up the beach, she had an overwhelming urge to call Flynn and find out what the procedure was for people leaving the islands on private boats. Staff were checking for anything suspicious at the airport and on the ferry, but it would be easy to get stolen goods out if you had your own yacht.

Or hitched a ride on someone else's.

Chapter Twenty-Three

NEEDING to address the feeling of discomfort which had been pestering Lily since her encounter with Len at the harbour, she set off for his place once the shop was closed for the day.

As she stood on his doorstep, he looked much calmer than when she'd last seen him, but his greeting definitely lacked his usual warmth.

"I know you probably don't want to see me." She spoke quickly, suspecting he might close the door in her face. "But I only want to say that I'm really sorry for this morning. I jumped to conclusions and I shouldn't have." She paused and when he didn't close the door on her, she bumbled on. "In my defence, I'd do the same thing again." She frowned. "Which I know makes my apology sound insincere, but I want to figure out who's been stealing and to do that I need to keep an open mind. I can't assume people are innocent because they seem like a nice person. I might make enemies but—"

He raised a hand, cutting her off. "I was angry this morning, but I've calmed down now. We're all good. You don't need to stand there yapping all evening. And if you're going to insist on your yapping, you should probably come in so the neighbours don't have to listen to you."

Relief had her whole body sagging. "I really am sorry," she said as she crossed the threshold.

"It's in the past." He gave her arm a pat, then led the way into the living room. "I didn't mean what I said about your windows either."

"Thank god," she said, flopping back onto the couch. "The only reason I came to grovel was the thought of having to clean them myself."

He chuckled, making his belly wobble. "I was upset this morning – having my honour called into question like that wasn't pleasant, but I soon calmed down. I think you and I are cut from the same cloth. We both care about this community and hate the thought of anyone taking advantage of people here. So I understand your wanting to catch this thief. Respect it even. You ask the hard questions, but anyone who's innocent won't hold that against you for long."

"Thanks for understanding."

"I tell you what I don't understand... what made you think it was me? Presumably because I'm a window cleaner and have access, but there must have been more than that."

"It's a long story," Lily said. "I thought it was someone at the art retreat to start with..." She spent ten minutes telling him about her investigations and making him laugh as she regaled him with the story of sneaking around Roland's room while he was fast asleep in bed.

"So as well as ruling me out as a suspect, you've also ruled out Roland?"

"Yes. But I'm not even convinced it's anything to do with the retreat any more so I'm probably just chasing my tail."

He lifted an eyebrow. "The pencil at the scene of the crime seems like a hefty clue to me."

She hadn't actually told Len about her missing items, but had claimed Hilary Phillips had found a pencil after the break in at her place. It felt good to chat it through, even if she still couldn't be completely open.

"Gideon told me he offers the pencils to everyone he meets," she said.

"That's true. I think he was going to suggest paying me in pencils once."

Lily laughed, but the mirth faded quickly. "I'm at a dead end," she said sulkily.

"It wouldn't surprise me if it were someone up at Gideon's place. They're an odd bunch from what I've seen." He pressed his head into the chair cushion. "Tell me what else you know. Maybe we can figure this out together."

Lily huffed out a breath. "I know Martha would like to leave her husband but feels tied to him because she isn't financially independent."

"That seems like a decent motive."

"Yes. But it doesn't feel right. She's so meek and mild. I can't imagine her turning to crime, no matter what the motive."

"What about that scruffy-looking fella?"

"Silas. He's an oddball, but I searched his tent and found nothing." She sat up straighter. "I guess the person I'm most suspicious of is Saffron."

"The hippy woman?"

Lily chuckled. "Yeah. She's changed her plans and is leaving tomorrow on a yacht. She got a job working as a nanny. Out of the blue, apparently. And I was thinking that if you were shifting stolen goods off the island, leaving on a private boat would be the easiest way to do it, wouldn't it?"

"The harbour master will keep an eye on private boats coming and going..." His voice trailed off, and he tilted his head.

"What are you thinking?" Lily asked.

"I'm thinking about my encounter with that hippy lady this morning."

"What encounter?"

"I sell things, don't I? Sometimes people ask me to sell items for them, and we split the money. Other times, people just give me their junk because they don't want the hassle of disposing of it."

"So?"

"Sometimes I sell stuff on the mainland, but I also sell things locally, on these online community groups."

"Are you going to get to the point anytime soon?"

He rolled his eyes. "Saffron bought a suitcase from me this morning."

"A suitcase?"

"Yeah. She said hers was worn out, and she needed an upgrade, but the one I sold her was pretty worn too."

Lily frowned, thinking. "Maybe she didn't need a new case, just an extra one..."

"She would if she were leaving with more than she arrived with," Len agreed with a slow nod.

"That seems as though it would be worth checking."

"I'd say so. Did she tell you what time she was leaving tomorrow?"

"No, but I have her phone number, and she seems to think we're firm friends, so I don't think it would seem odd if I asked her."

"Do that. Then let your copper friend know where to find her..."

"Yeah."

"Or I can give Sergeant Proctor a call if you'd rather?"

"No." She shook her head. "I'll be seeing Flynn later anyway, so I'll talk to him about it."

Chapter Twenty-Four

In a sleep-deprived trance, Flynn didn't notice the sergeant enter the station late in the afternoon until he was all the way inside.

"I spent an hour wandering the town, but it's all quiet," the sergeant mused, easing into the chair behind the other desk. "Maybe our thief is having a day in bed after their nighttime activities."

"Lucky him," Flynn said through a yawn. "It's odd though, that they didn't actually commit any crimes yesterday evening."

"By the sounds of it, they didn't have the chance – what with you and Lily chasing around, and half the island awake and keeping watch."

Flynn yawned again. "It still feels a bit off to me."

"You don't think it was the thief?"

"My gut says no."

"Just someone out for a midnight stroll?" the sergeant asked, scepticism clear in his tone.

"I dunno," Flynn said.

"You look done in," the sergeant said. "Go home and get some sleep."

"Do you want me patrolling tonight?"

"No. It's definitely my turn. And I promise not to leave my phone downstairs when I go to bed tonight." He gave an exaggerated sigh. "I still can't believe I did that. I always have my phone by my bed. Every single night. I put it there on autopilot. I've no idea what happened last night."

"Don't worry about it." Flynn leaned back in his chair. "And I'm happy to patrol again tonight... I'd just need to get a power nap in first."

He fully expected the sergeant to turn him down and was a little concerned when he looked thoughtful. Flynn actually wanted to spend the evening with Lily. Although, at the rate he was yawning, he was probably only fit for sleep. He could have a nap, though. He'd be fine after a nap.

"No," the sergeant said eventually. "You need a night off. Thanks for the offer."

"Are you still not feeling well?" Flynn asked.

"I feel as though I could do with a holiday. Maybe I'm just envious of PC Hill. A break sounds pretty good."

Flynn was working up the energy to leave, but paused. "My flight is booked for next Saturday." It felt surreal that he'd be leaving in barely more than a week.

The sergeant nodded. "You said. Are we going to have drinks before you leave? Seren was saying something about organising a do in the Mermaid Inn..."

Flynn shook his head. "She mentioned it to me, but I told her not to bother. I don't want any fanfare. The thought of leaving is hard enough as it is. I'm still hoping the powers that be will decide I'm needed here long term."

"I do think I'm making headway," the sergeant said. "It's not going to happen before the end of next week, though."

"Yeah, I know. I'd just rather we save the drinks for when I'm back here with a permanent job on St Mary's."

The sergeant nodded sagely. "I like the sound of that."

. . .

Twenty minutes later, Flynn grumbled to himself when he pushed open the door of the ice cream shop and got no resistance. The sign was turned to closed, and the place was empty.

"Hi," Lily called from the back room.

"You should lock the door," he said, the words coming out more harshly than he intended. "There's a criminal on the loose in case you haven't heard."

Given the mess on every available work surface in the back, it appeared that Lily was at various stages of making several batches of ice cream.

"You look worn out," she said, ignoring his nagging.

"You look busy." He frowned at the chaotic room. "I was hoping we could grab dinner and chill out for the evening."

"By chill out do you mean pass out on the couch, because that looks about all you're fit for."

He dragged a hand through his hair. "How do you look so perky? You can't have got much more sleep than me."

"No, but you also haven't had much sleep for a few nights in a row."

"True. Why are you making so much ice cream? I thought things had been quieter?"

"Yeah." A muscle twitched in her cheek, and he could've sworn she looked guilty. "I just have a bunch of fresh ingredients I need to use up. From now on, Sally won't deliver so much, but she had berries and herbs that she didn't want to go to waste."

He stretched his neck and looked thoughtful. "How long is this going to take?"

"A couple of hours at least."

"Should I help you?"

"That's about the most half-hearted offer I've ever heard."

His lips pulled into a smile. "Sorry. I'm kind of done in."

"Go home and sleep," she said. "I'll see you tomorrow."

"I can stay and help if you want."

"It's fine."

"I can go for a nap for a couple of hours and then we can do something."

"That won't happen, and we both know it."

"I'll set an alarm. Or you can just come and wake me up when you're finished here..." Now that was an appealing plan. Waking from a nap would be a lot easier if she crawled into bed with him.

She didn't look at him, and he could've sworn she was searching for an excuse.

"Let's do something tomorrow instead," she said quietly.

He moved closer, a hand slipping around her waist. "What's going on?"

"Nothing." She leaned her head back, snuggling into his chest. "I'm tired as well, and I just think I'll be wiped out by the time I'm finished here."

He brought his other arm around her, pinning her to his chest and inhaling the citrusy scent of her shampoo. "You can talk to me, you know?" he whispered against her forehead.

Her voice was a barely audible squeak. "What?"

"I feel as though you have a lot on your mind. I don't know if it's the stuff with Maria, or if it's me leaving, but I think you'd feel better if you talked instead of bottling it up."

"I'm not," she said, but her brittle voice gave it away as a lie.

"Okay," he said, pressing a kiss to her hairline. "But if there's something bothering you, I always have time to listen." He loosened his grip, but she clutched at his arms, holding him in place.

Only for a moment, then she inhaled dramatically and moved away.

"If you don't leave me to get on with this, I'll never finish." She gave him a peck, then turned away, focusing on her work.

He lingered for a moment, watching her fold blackberries into the ice cream.

Then he forced himself to leave, hoping she found whatever comfort she needed in her ice cream making.

Chapter Twenty-Five

The harbour was getting busy when Lily ventured down there bright and early, keeping an eye out for Saffron. She'd kept things chatty when she'd messaged her the previous evening – commenting on how lovely it had been to meet her and wishing her well, before casually asking what time she'd be leaving.

Seeing her arrive at the harbour, Lily pulled her cap down to keep her face in shadow. Saffron dragged two tattered suitcases on wheels. Which meant she'd lied to Len about needing an upgrade. Apparently, she'd needed more space in her luggage.

A man in chinos and a polo shirt approached and gave her a warm hug before taking the larger of the cases down the harbour steps for her.

There was no rush, Lily coached herself. They wouldn't set sail immediately. She could hang back for a few minutes at least.

The hi-vis vest balled in her hand was a thin, gauzy material. Nothing heavy duty – more like something a cyclist would wear. It had been sitting in the lost property box at the ice cream shop for weeks, and she was certain whoever lost it wasn't coming back for it.

She slipped it on as she descended the harbour steps. Surely any volunteer worth their salt wore some sort of high visibility clothing.

On the jetty, she headed quickly for the sailing boat Saffron had boarded.

"Morning!" she called confidently when she got near.

"Hello!" Saffron said. "What are you doing here?"

"Official business, I'm afraid." She directed her words at the man and cast a quick smile at the woman and two little girls standing beside him.

"Is there a problem?" the man asked.

"No problem," she said. "But the police are stretched thin at the moment, so they've enlisted volunteers to help with a few things. I'm not sure if you know that there has been a spate of thefts recently."

The woman nodded. "The harbour master spoke to us about it when we arrived yesterday. Told us to be aware and let us know of anyone acting oddly."

"We're all being extra careful," Lily said. "Any kind of suspicious activity is being looked into." She cast Saffron an apologetic glance and remembered what Len had said about people being forgiving if they were innocent. "Unfortunately, your last-minute change in travel plans has raised a red flag. It's absolutely not a big deal, and I don't want to hold you up any longer than necessary, but I have to ask you to submit to a voluntary search of your belongings. If you'd rather the police do it, you're welcome to wait for them, but we'd need to ask that you don't leave the islands until that time."

Saffron pressed her lips together. "I'm under suspicion?"

"This is all routine," Lily said calmly. "I hope you won't take any offence."

"Oh, gosh," the woman said, a hand pressed to her sternum. "I can promise you the last-minute change of plans was entirely spontaneous. We weren't even planning to stop here, but then I saw Saffron's advert, and it wasn't much of a detour. If you think this is some elaborate plan..."

"She didn't say that," the man said. "She's only doing her job. Saffron, can she check your bags so we can leave as planned?"

Saffron twirled the end of her plait around her finger. "I suppose it's fine." She glanced at her bags. "Everything is well packed though. If I open it here, there'll be an explosion of clothes."

"We can go down into your cabin if you'd prefer," Lily said.

"That's probably better." She picked up one of the bags, and Lily took the other.

Silently, they lugged them through the galley and into a cosy cabin.

"This is bad," Saffron said, as soon as she closed the door behind them. "Very bad."

"What is?" A chill raced up Lily's spine as she recalled the last time she'd been in the cabin of a yacht and had ended up stowed away in a wardrobe.

"Would it be okay if you didn't search my bags? You could just say you did. We are friends after all. You could just trust that I didn't steal anything. I could give you my word. That should be enough between friends."

"Did you steal something?" Lily asked, the cabin feeling suddenly smaller as Saffron blocked the door.

"No." She chewed on the end of her plait. "But sometimes the universe offers me things, and I have to accept them. I don't want to risk causing offence."

"To the universe?"

"Yes."

Lily swallowed hard. "I really have to check your bags. I'm sorry."

"That's going to be very awkward," she said, her tone slightly menacing.

Lily took an instinctive step back as Saffron came towards her. She reminded herself that she could handle herself in a physical altercation.

"Please don't judge me too harshly." Saffron stopped before

Lily and lifted the bag at her feet to heft it onto the bed. The whir of the zip filled the room before she threw back the lid of the suitcase. "Gideon gave it to me. I swear I didn't steal anything. You can ask him yourself if you don't believe me."

"What the heck is all of this?" Lily lifted a Ziploc bag filled with assorted cutlery, and then another filled with Gideon's pencils advertising the art retreat. Her eyes darted to a stainless-steel pan and what appeared to be plates protected by bubble wrap. There were tea towels and a frilly tablecloth, and most of it looked as though it could have gone into the bin.

"He said he was having a clear out and he kept offering things. I can't say no to free stuff – the universe might think I'm ungrateful and stop offering it."

With a quick shake of her head, Lily moved the case aside. "I need to check the other bag too."

Saffron emptied it out, shaking it until the bed was no longer visible beneath the mound of clothes and scarves and toiletries.

"Can we still be friends?" Saffron asked once Lily had rummaged through it. "You don't think I'm a weirdo, do you?"

"No," Lily said, because what was one more lie on top of all the others she'd told in the last week? "I'm just glad you're not a thief."

And that she'd eliminated one more suspect.

Chapter Twenty-Six

Lily spotted Martha standing at the top of Porthcressa Beach when she returned to the ice cream shop. She had her phone to her ear, and Lily contemplated whether she could sneak close enough to eavesdrop, but just as she was pondering it, Martha turned and spotted her. She waved and gave a weak smile.

No eavesdropping this morning then.

Frustrated by her lack of current leads, she continued to the shop.

With Saffron off her list of suspects, that left Martha and Silas. If it was someone from the retreat, anyway. She didn't like to think too much about that because if it wasn't someone connected to the retreat, she really was at a dead end.

Her gut told her Martha was her most likely suspect.

Just as she stepped inside the ice cream shop, her phone rang, and she sighed before answering the call from Len.

"What happened with Saffron?" he asked. "Did the police question her?"

"No." She swallowed hard as she moved back outside. "I went to talk to her myself. She let me search her things."

"And?"

"It wasn't her."

"You're sure? Why did she need a new suitcase?"

"Gideon had been giving her random things from his house, and she won't say no to free stuff. There was so much that she needed an extra suitcase for it."

"You're sure it wasn't stolen goods."

"If she'd stolen this stuff, I'd say she did someone a favour. It was a load of old junk. Pots and pans and random household items."

"That's a bit of a letdown. I thought with our combined information we'd cracked the case."

"I'm afraid not."

"What's your next move then?"

"I don't know. I was thinking of questioning Martha, and maybe Silas. It all feels futile, though. I'm missing something, I'm sure of it."

"What about Gideon?"

She bobbed her head from side to side. "I don't know what to think."

"What do you usually do when you're investigating?"

"Mostly just keep bothering people and snooping around until I hit on something useful."

"That's what you should do then." His enthusiasm gave Lily a burst of positivity. "Need any help?" he asked.

"No. Thanks. I think I'll try talking to Martha again."

"Good idea. Let me know if anything comes of it."

She promised she would and ended the call.

Wandering across the promenade, she looked out across the sand, but Martha was nowhere in sight. She'd been there a few minutes ago.

Frowning, Lily went back into the shop and began taking the tables and chairs outside while trying to decide on the best course of action.

Maybe she could be completely forthcoming with Martha. After all, if she'd been stealing from people, she did it with good reason. It didn't make it okay, but Lily could at least have a little sympathy.

She could ask her outright and make a deal with her. If she handed over the rest of the stolen goods and Lily's passports, she could keep Lily's money. It was enough for her to start a new life. Lily could wait until Martha had left and then leave the recovered goods at the police station door. Everyone would get their stuff back, Martha would get her fresh start, and Lily could burn her fake passport and stop worrying about it being discovered.

The idea percolated as she set out the ice cream trays in the display cabinet.

A knock at the door had her looking up. Martha had a takeaway mug from Pippa's cafe in her hand as she gingerly pushed at the handle.

"I know you're not really open yet, but I wondered if you might have time for a little chat."

"Come in," Lily said. "I was hoping I'd catch you again."

"I wanted to share my news with someone, but Saffron has already left."

"What news?" Lily nodded at a table, and they sat opposite each other.

"I'm going to leave my husband."

"Wow." Lily said, trying to come up with an appropriate response while really wondering why she suddenly felt able to leave him after so many years.

"I've been on the phone to my sister for the last hour. She's over the moon. She said she's been worried about me for years, and she's been so supportive." Tears filled Martha's eyes, and she pulled a tissue from her pocket. "I don't think I'd be brave enough if it weren't for Janet. It's so scary to think of losing financial support. I might not have been happy with Gregory, but I always knew I had a warm house and hot meals. There's security in that which you tend not to think about until it's in jeopardy."

"That's true," Lily said. "How will you manage financially, if you don't mind my asking?"

"I don't know." More tears welled on her lower lids. "I have my pension, which I can divert into my secret account." She sniffed loudly. "It won't need to be a secret any more I suppose, just my private account. He can't touch that."

"Is your pension enough to live on?"

"No. Not really. But my sister insisted I go and live with her. She said not to worry about money, but I'll hate being a burden on her, so I'll try to find myself a little job. Nothing too stressful. Maybe once I'm feeling more settled, I'll get a lawyer and see about a divorce, and try to get what I'm owed from my marriage. That's what Janet says I should do, but I'm just feeling too delicate at the moment to even think about it. I need to get my confidence back."

"Yes." Lily forced a smile, feeling once again as though she'd hit a wall in her investigation. Martha really didn't seem like someone who'd recently come into a large stash of cash.

After checking her watch, Martha stood. "I have to get going. We're going to spend a few hours painting on the beach."

"That sounds very soothing."

"Yes. Although, it won't be the same without Saffron. She's a bit of a funny thing, but I enjoyed spending time with her. I don't have quite the same connection to the men in the group. Roland is nice enough, but I struggle with Silas. We don't have much in common." She smiled. "He's had us in stitches though with his tree climbing. I don't know if he thinks we can't see him down at the end of the garden, but he's up and down that tree like a monkey. It's bizarre!"

"That is weird." Lily chewed her lower lip. "Enjoy your afternoon," she said as Martha left.

Maybe she hadn't been barking up the wrong tree by investigating the art retreat after all. Perhaps she just hadn't been thinking literally enough when considering which tree to bark up.

Chapter Twenty-Seven

Craning her neck, Lily stared up at the oak tree by Silas's tent and wondered how she got herself into such ridiculous situations. After another quick glance around to check the coast was clear, she reached for the first branch, which hung a little above head height. Thankfully, she had good upper body strength, or she'd never have made it up that first bit. From there, a few branches were closer together and she scrambled higher with ease.

Then she stopped to catch her breath and scan the branches. It would be quite a brilliant place to hide stuff. If it weren't for Silas being seen climbing the tree, it would never have occurred to her to search in a tree. With no sign of anything, she suspected her theory was a little too far on the wild side, but continued higher. As the branches thinned out again, she curled her fingers into a hole in the trunk to see if she could use it to haul herself higher.

Her fingers brushed against something. Instinctively, she reached further in and fumbled around until she had a firm hold on what felt like a plastic bag.

"Bingo!" she said triumphantly, eyeing the clear plastic bag filled with cash.

A quick flick through the notes told her it was almost a thousand pounds. On a rush of adrenaline, she shoved the package into the back pocket of her cutoff jeans and circled the tree trunk, looking for further hidey-holes. Finding a convenient branch, she ventured higher before setting off down again, her hands and eyes searching every inch of the tree.

"Hey!"

The angry voice came loudly and out of the blue.

Startled, Lily's foot slipped, and for one excruciating second, time slowed. She grasped at branches that she couldn't quite grip.

Then everything went incredibly fast. The skin on her leg burned as it scraped along the bark of a thick branch. The same sensation ripped across her arm and then her face. Something crashed into her side, and she had the fleeting image of a pinball being flung around a machine.

Bang, bang, bang.

Thud, thud, thud.

She had absolutely no control.

Just when she expected to hit the ground, she felt warm skin instead.

And then the ground.

Silas swore loudly while she breathed in the scent of soil and grass.

"I couldn't catch you," he said. "But I broke your fall at least. Are you okay? Are you alive?"

It took her a moment to peel herself off the ground.

"I'm alive," she said, spitting out a blade of grass and gingerly touching her face, then checking her fingers. "No blood," she murmured. "Just a graze then?"

"A lot of grazes," Silas said, eyes wide as he stared at her calf and then her upper arm. "You're pretty banged up. Is anything broken?"

"Don't think so," she said, checking each limb as she eased herself to a sitting position.

"I'd call 999 but I don't have a phone."

Lily twisted herself to look at her shoulder, which was all scraped up. "I don't need an ambulance."

"I was going to call the police, not an ambulance."

She flinched when he reached down, but he only plucked the bag of cash from the ground beside her.

"You were stealing my stuff," he growled.

"How can I steal it from you when it's not yours?"

"Of course it's mine."

Lily rubbed the back of her head, feeling a bump rising. "Listen, can you please just give me my backpack? I won't make a fuss. Keep my money for all I care." She'd set the police on him later but she wasn't about to tell him that. "I just need the passports."

"Have you got a concussion?" Silas asked.

"Possibly, but can you please give me the passports?"

He glanced around, and Lily felt a spark of hope.

"I can run back to the beach and get one of them to call an ambulance. I think you need medical attention."

"I don't."

"You're talking gibberish."

"I'm not. You stole my backpack, and I need you to return it."

He shook his head. "I've just caught you up a tree stealing my money, but you're claiming *I'm* a thief?"

"Yes. It's not your money. Why would you keep your money in a tree unless you were trying to hide something?"

"Because I live in a tent." He pointed at it. "It's not exactly secure, and I heard there's a thief terrorising the island, so I hid my money in the tree."

Lily inhaled deeply. "That actually makes sense." She rubbed her forehead. "I thought you were skint. Why not stay in the guest accommodation if you have all that money?"

"Because it wouldn't last very long if I were paying a couple of hundred quid a night to sleep inside."

"That's true," Lily said. "But surely it would be more secure to keep your money in the bank."

"I'd argue with you on that, but I find the conversation isn't a lot of fun."

"Okay." She took another deep breath and stood up, testing to see if any of the pain was more than just scrapes and bruises. "So you didn't steal anything?"

"No." He looked at his money, then took it from the bag and counted it. "You weren't trying to steal from me?"

"No. I want to catch the thief."

"They stole from you?"

"Yeah."

"Did you tell the police?"

"No."

"That's why you've been hanging around here so much? You think one of us is the thief?"

"I *did*, yes. Now I'm not so sure."

He put the money back in the bag. "If I hide this in the same spot, can you please not tell anyone where it is?"

"I won't say anything, but people saw you climbing the tree, so if you want to be really secure, you might want a new hiding spot."

"I'll just keep it on me for now." He lifted his shirt and shoved the cash into his bumbag. "I only came back for a jumper. They're waiting for me back at the beach."

"Don't let me keep you," she said as she hobbled towards the house.

Silas ducked into his tent, then walked quickly past her.

"Sorry for scaring you."

She nodded. "Thanks for breaking my fall."

At the fire pit, she sank down onto the ground, resting against a log while she worked up the energy to get herself home.

Chapter Twenty-Eight

Lily hadn't moved when a message came through from Flynn, asking how her day was going.

It was difficult to know how to reply to that. Telling him she'd fallen out of a tree and been ravaged by every branch on the way down would raise a lot of questions.

Saying her day was going well would be a pretty juicy lie.

Fine, she wrote in the end. A definite twist of the truth, but compared to some people's day it might seem all right. Though she'd certainly feel sorry for those poor people.

Busy? he asked.

Yeah.

Me too. Talk to you later.

She sent him a row of kisses and shoved her phone back into her pocket, wincing at the movement.

The phone vibrated again immediately, and she groaned as she pulled it out. Len's name flashed on the screen.

"Just wanted to check in," he said when she answered. "Any new developments in the case?"

"I keep hitting dead ends," she said, relieved at being able to talk about it.

"What have you found out?"

"I've ruled out all the guests at the retreat."

"Oh." He sounded disappointed. "Where do we go from here then?"

She smiled at his use of 'we' – as though they were in it together.

"I don't know. It seems I've probably been looking in the wrong place all along. Anyone could have dropped that pencil at Hilary's place."

"It seems odd, though. Even if lots of people have the pencils, most people wouldn't carry them around, would they? Not unless they'd only just been given it."

"What should I do, ask Gideon for a list of everyone he's given them out to?"

"Good luck with that. The man is utterly chaotic. I can't imagine he remembers who he's given them to."

"What do you mean he's chaotic?"

"He's a bit of a wool gatherer sometimes. Also, if you saw the state of his place, you'd know exactly what I mean by chaotic. Not that I'm one to talk."

"I've seen it, actually."

He gave a surprised grunt. "He doesn't usually let anyone in."

"I kind of barged in. I wanted to look for the stolen goods, but I didn't get further than the hallway before he marched me out again. That's actually the only part of the retreat I haven't searched." She paused. "Does he let you in there?"

"No. I just see in through the windows when I'm cleaning."

"Oh." She hadn't thought about him doing the windows at that side of the house.

As she struggled to get off the floor, she let out an involuntary whimper.

"Are you okay?" Len asked.

"Yeah." She breathed deeply through her nose until the pain subsided.

"Are you sure? It sounded as though you were crying."

"I just... I have a slight injury but I'm fine." She half walked, half staggered around the back of the house. "The window is open," she stated.

"What did you say?"

"Gideon left a window open at the back."

"You're at his place?"

"Yes. I thought maybe Silas was stashing stolen goods in the tree, but he's not. I was about to leave when you rang."

"What were you saying about an open window?"

"I was thinking I could nip in and have a quick look around, but the window's high, and I've done as much climbing as I can manage today. I don't think I'll make it up the drainpipe."

"If only you knew a guy with a ladder," he said mockingly.

Lily's mind raced. With a ladder, it would be easy to get inside for a poke around.

"I assume no one is there?" Len asked.

"No, they're painting on a beach somewhere."

"Do you know when they're due back?"

"From what Martha said, I guess not for an hour at least. Maybe two."

"Plenty of time then. I'm on my way now. I'll be five minutes."

Lily started to speak, but the line had gone dead. She wasn't sure what she wanted to say anyway, but she had her thoughts in order by the time Len's van pulled onto the drive.

He got straight to work getting the ladder off the roof, then carried it on his shoulder round the back of the house while Lily limped along beside him.

"I'm not sure about this," she said.

"I thought it was the only place you hadn't looked."

"It is, but climbing in through an upstairs window seems like crossing a line. Usually, when I sneak into places, it's through unlocked doors, or onto boats and stuff. This feels like taking things too far."

"It won't take long. We can be in and out before anyone

notices. And if Gideon happens to come back, I can say I got confused about my cleaning schedule."

"I don't know." She swallowed hard while he lined his ladder up beside the open window.

With a hand on a rung, he turned to look at her and flinched.

"Blooming heck, Lily. What happened to you?"

"It's nothing."

"It doesn't look like nothing. It looks as though you..."

"Fell out of a tree?" she suggested.

"That wouldn't have been my first guess, but now that you mention it." He smiled sympathetically. "Do you need to see a doctor? We can give up on this plan, and I'll drive you to the medical centre."

"No. I'm okay. I don't know if we should break into his house, but I don't need a doctor."

"You might be right that we're going too far. Did I get carried away?"

"I think so. Which is weird because it's usually me that dives headfirst into these sorts of crazy schemes."

He nodded repeatedly. "I think I just got caught up in the idea of catching the thief."

"It's probably not Gideon anyway. He has no motive for robbing locals."

"Apart from being resentful that he has to live here and entertain wannabe artists instead of living an artist's dream in London as he'd like to. But if you don't consider that... and his bitterness that no one here buys his artwork... set all that aside and I can't think of any motive whatsoever."

"But he chose to live here. He likes the tranquillity."

"Codswallop! He came back from London with his tail between his legs because he couldn't make a living there. No one was interested in his art there, any more than they are here."

"That's not what he told me."

"That's hardly a surprise. Every man has his pride." He

moved to pull the ladder away from the wall. "Let's get out of here before anyone catches us."

Lily stopped him with a hand on the ladder. "I could have a really quick look," she said, her foot already on the first rung. "You wait out here and keep watch."

Ignoring the pain that throbbed along the entire right side of her body, she climbed the ladder as quickly as possible. The large window was easy to step through, though she knocked a small cactus off the windowsill when she climbed in. Quickly, she scooped the spilled soil back into the pot and dispersed the rest with her shoe.

She got a shock when she straightened up to find Len at the top of the ladder.

"I thought you were keeping watch," she said, her voice instinctively quiet.

"We'll be quicker if we both look. Besides, I don't want you taking all the credit if it turns out that Gideon is the thief." He flashed her a playful grin and shot across the kitchen. "You check in here. I'll make a start on the bedroom."

Working with an accomplice felt odd, and she didn't love being told what to do, but she got straight to work anyway, rifling through drawers and cupboards.

Finding nothing, her gaze swept over the assorted junk in the room. The backpack shouldn't be too difficult to spot.

With nothing obvious in the kitchen, she headed into the hallway.

"Any luck?" she whisper-hissed to Len.

"Nothing yet," he replied.

Lily moved into the small living room and sighed at the mess. "How would you even tell if there were stolen goods?" she muttered. "At least he probably won't notice if we leave something out of place."

"What was that?" Len asked, appearing beside her, apparently thinking she'd been talking to him.

"I don't even know where to start." The piles of books and

magazines were all over the place, some seeming to act as tables with a glass or mug balanced on top.

Her eyes went to the side of the couch where the sunlight reflected off a shiny object on the floor.

"Look at that," she whispered, crouching to look at the necklace.

Len loomed beside her. "How are we supposed to know if that's stolen property or just more of his junk?"

Lily squinted, trying to get a better look at the pendant without touching the necklace. "I think Hilary said the one taken from her place was a silver heart with a blue stone."

"Is that a silver heart?" Len asked.

"Yes. But that doesn't mean it's Hilary's."

"Why not send her a photo and ask?"

Lily straightened up and felt another jolt of pain. "Because if she knows we found it, she'll expect us to return it. But we can't do that since we're not supposed to be here."

"What was your plan then? For if we found something?"

She rubbed the bump on her head. "I have a habit of not thinking things through that far. Hang on a second..." She paced the room while she pondered it, then she pulled out her phone. "I'll ask Hilary to describe the necklace. I think she said she'd given the police a photo, so maybe she can give me that." The woman had talked so much that Lily hadn't taken it all in, but she had a vague notion that she'd mentioned a photo.

"What do we do if it's hers?"

She tapped on her phone, messaging Hilary. "Nothing for now. We leave it here, get out and don't mention to anyone we were here. Then we'll give the police an anonymous tip so they come and search."

Len beamed. "You're very good at this."

"Thank you." Her phone pinged, and she opened the message from Hilary, which included a photo of the stolen necklace. She zoomed in.

"It's Hilary's necklace," she said after checking the one on the floor again. "I don't want to touch it, but I'd like to move it so Gideon doesn't spot it..." She nudged it with the toe of her shoe so it was a little more hidden by the stack of books. "Gideon must have dropped it there by accident. I'm sure the rest of his stash isn't far away." Her eyes darted around the room. If she could just get her hands on her backpack, she could put all this behind her.

"Time to go?" Len asked.

"Yes," Lily replied. "I'm right behind you." She went to the kitchen with him as though she intended to follow him right out. Instead, she waited until he was a couple of rungs down before she told him she just wanted to check something and darted back through the kitchen.

The backpack must be around somewhere. But as she scrambled through every inch of the living room and then the bedroom, she began to lose hope. Maybe there was an attic space. She couldn't see anything obvious, though. Or perhaps there was a cellar.

"Lily!" Len hissed from outside. "Hurry up."

"I'm coming," she muttered dejectedly. Climbing back down felt like way more effort than going up. Partly because she was losing hope of ever finding her backpack and partly because her battered muscles were becoming stiffer by the minute.

"Sorry," Len said when she was safely on the ground. "I thought I heard someone, but I think it was just hikers passing on the lane. Let's get out of here. I'm getting twitchy now. I'll drive you home."

"I'd appreciate that," she said, hobbling back to the van beside Len and his ladder.

"What happens now?" he asked on the drive across the island. "Should I leave everything to you?"

"Yes. Leave it to me," she said wearily. She whipped her head up abruptly. "I know you were joking earlier about me getting the credit, but we really can't ever tell anyone what we just did. It's totally illegal. Also, it will be bad for business if people think you've been using your ladder to climb in people's windows and trespass on their property. Even if Gideon is guilty."

"Do you have any doubts about that?"

"The evidence is right there in his flat. But it won't make any difference. Even if it was for a good cause, people won't like what we did."

"You're right, of course. I'll have to settle for being an unsung hero of this tale."

She smiled lightly. "Sometimes that's just the way it goes."

Chapter Twenty-Nine

LEN DROPPED her off as close to the ice cream shop as he could get, but she quickly decided on a change of destination. Once she'd cleaned herself up, all she'd want to do is lie on the couch in her pyjamas and not venture out again.

Hobbling through Hugh Town, she got a few odd looks. Apparently, her injuries weren't subtle.

Pulling out her phone, she called Flynn.

"Are you at the station?" she asked.

"Yeah."

"Can you meet me outside in about two minutes?"

"You could just come in," he said, a quizzical note in his voice.

"I could, but I'd rather not. Come outside, please."

He'd just walked out when she rounded the corner. The sympathetic tilt of his head made her want to snuggle against his chest and cry until she felt better.

"What happened?" he asked softly.

"I fell out of a tree." She'd have laughed, but suspected that would hurt.

Flynn's eyebrows lifted. "Should I ask?"

"Not right now. I have other stuff to tell you about. This little anecdote can wait."

"Are you okay, though?"

"Nothing's broken." That didn't seem to reassure him, but she continued anyway. "I did something today that I can't tell you about, but I have information for you about the person responsible for the thefts."

He opened his mouth, then closed it again. "What information?" he finally asked.

"You should search Gideon Rowe's place. Not just the communal spaces but his private rooms upstairs. The ones he always keeps locked."

"Should I assume we'll find the stolen goods there?"

She nodded.

"And how do you know this?"

"I can't tell you."

"Because you did something you shouldn't have?"

"Yeah."

"Something illegal?"

"Yes. But with the best of intentions."

"Okay." He paused, thinking. "I don't see why we can't ask him to submit to a voluntary search. Especially since his place is so close to Hilary Phillip's house." He looked suddenly pensive. "He wasn't there," he said wistfully.

She put a hand to the back of her head, wondering if Silas had been right about her having a concussion since his words were confusing her. "What are you talking about?"

"I went up to the retreat the night of the break in. The guests were all sitting around outside, but I didn't see Gideon."

"He was also at Porthcressa Beach when..." Lily caught herself and stopped.

"When what?"

She tipped her head back and blew out a breath. "I need you to do something for me."

"What?"

"When you find the stolen goods, you'll find a black backpack. It has a little blue flower embroidered on the front pocket, and it belongs to me. I need you to get it back for me."

His eyebrows drew together. "They stole something from you too?"

"Yes. I left the doors open when I went for a run the other morning, and when I got back, my backpack was gone." Emotions collected in her throat, making talking difficult. "I didn't tell you because I thought I could get it back myself."

"What's in it?"

"I can't tell you."

"Something illegal?"

She couldn't answer that because she didn't know the answer. "It's personal stuff that belonged to my uncle. I found it in his flat after he died." Tears collected on her lower lids. "I need you to get it back for me. Without letting the sergeant look inside the bag, and without looking in it yourself."

"Okay," he said after a moment.

"*Okay*?" Was that it? No more questions?

"If I find it, I'll get it back to you." He reached for her hand, lifting it to inspect the grazes on her arm. "You need to clean this. It's got dirt in it."

"I know, I haven't been home yet." The conversation had moved on too quickly, and she wasn't convinced he'd got the message, or that he was taking her seriously. "I really need you to get the backpack to me without anyone looking through it."

"I heard you," he said impatiently. "But if you get sepsis because you don't clean these wounds properly, your backpack won't matter much."

"I'm going home for a bath."

"Make sure all these cuts and scrapes are clean and dry. And cover them. Do you have plasters? Big ones?"

"Yes."

"Ask Jessica to help you if you can't reach the ones on your shoulder."

"Can you stop fussing now, please?"

He nodded. "I'd give you a hug but I'm scared of hurting you."

Disappointment had her lips turning down.

"I'll hug you if you want," he said, palms raised.

"No, I just realised we'll need to postpone our evening plans again."

"True." He grimaced as his eyes trailed down the length of her. "That's not an attractive look."

"Flynn!" She swatted at his chest. "I meant because I'm in pain, not because I look gross."

"Yeah. That's absolutely what I said, wasn't it?"

"No." She pouted, but leaned into him with her good side and slipped an arm around his waist.

"I can drive you home," he said.

"I thought you weren't allowed to take me in the police car."

"Not when I'm going to an incident. When you *are* the incident, it's a different matter."

She snorted a laugh, then shook her head. "I can manage. You need to deal with Gideon."

Chapter Thirty

FLYNN TRIED to call Lily when he left Gideon's place that evening. And then later, when he'd tied things up back at the station, and went home for the evening.

She didn't answer, and he hoped that meant she'd cleaned herself up and gone to bed early.

But he also really needed to speak to her. The events of the day swirled in his head when he finally got into bed.

He woke to a message from her saying she'd fallen asleep early – just as he'd suspected. Rushing to get ready for work, he only called her when he was about to leave. With his phone to his ear, he took a seat on the couch, figuring he could finish his coffee while he spoke to her.

"What happened?" she asked, answering almost immediately.

"Not a lot."

"You didn't find anything?"

"We found a necklace that belongs to Hilary Phillips."

"Is that all?"

"Yes. We searched every inch of the place, but that's the only thing we found."

"Okay. He must have a hiding place elsewhere."

"We did a thorough search," he said, his words clipped. "And from what we understand, Gideon doesn't have a lot of friends or family on the island, so I don't think it's likely he left it with someone else."

"I don't understand."

"Neither do I, but I need to ask you something..."

"What?"

He pressed his fingers into his temples. "I need to know if the forensic team is likely to find your fingerprints on that necklace."

There, he'd said it.

She didn't respond.

"I'm sorry," he said, without sounding the least bit heartfelt. "But you've been acting really strange, and you won't tell me what's going on, so I just need you to tell me this. Will your fingerprints be on that necklace?"

"No," she said quietly.

"Because you've never touched it, or because you were careful not to leave fingerprints on it?"

"I've never touched it."

"Good." He released a sigh.

"What exactly do you think I've been doing?"

His jaw tightened. "I've absolutely no idea. That's the problem."

She fell silent for a moment, then chose not to address his remark. "Gideon's fingerprints will be on the necklace," she said.

"I'll actually be amazed if they are."

"Why?"

"Because he didn't hesitate about letting us search the place, and he seemed genuinely surprised when we found the necklace. He swears he's never seen it before and doesn't know how it got there."

"Of course he'd say that."

"It's not *what he said,*" Flynn snapped. "It's the way he said it. He was very believable. And he was keen that we get the necklace to forensics to prove he's never touched it."

"That only means he was careful."

"He also has an alibi for the night Hilary Phillips was burgled."

"You said he wasn't at the retreat."

"I said I didn't see him there. But the others say he was there all evening, sitting in the studio. He was on a video call with a couple of friends in London and came out to shout at the people on the retreat for being too loud when he was on the call. They say they had eyes on him through the window all evening. His friends in London also corroborate his story."

"That can't be right."

"I think you've got the wrong person."

"No," Lily said. "There's no one else. It has to be him."

Flynn downed the dregs of his coffee. "I have to get to work."

"How long will the forensic report take?"

"Who knows – probably a couple of days at least."

He ended the call and set off for the station. As he wandered along Garrison Lane, he passed Len Marrack going the other way.

"What are you selling today?" he asked, smiling at the window cleaner and tipping his head at the large box he wheeled along.

"Pressure washer," he said, smiling widely. "Always wheeling and dealing, I am!"

"It seems like it." Flynn told him to have a good day and continued to the station.

"You look confused," the sergeant said when he walked inside.

He didn't speak as he continued to puzzle things out in his mind.

"Flynn!" the sergeant snapped.

"Sorry. I just had a thought."

"And that was a bit too much exertion, was it?"

Flynn chuckled. "Have you got a screwdriver?"

"There's a toolkit in the back. Why?"

"Because I suspect Gideon Rowe had nothing to do with the thefts. I think someone planted the necklace at his place so we'd focus on him. In the meantime, the actual thief can move the stolen goods off the island while we're busy looking at Gideon."

"And you need a screwdriver, because?"

"I need to take a pressure washer apart to prove my theory."

Chapter Thirty-One

Hazy clouds diluted the sunlight as Lily lifted the tables and chairs outside to set up the shop. She should probably go for a run, but was lacking motivation. Besides, her injuries from the previous day were a good enough excuse to avoid physical activity for the day.

She'd expected to wake stiff and sore, but it wasn't as bad as she anticipated. Long trousers and a shirt covered most of it, and the few scratches along her jaw and neck weren't as dramatic once she'd cleaned them.

When Kit waved at her from the end of the promenade, she set off wandering in his direction. She only spotted Seren when she got close, tucked away on a bench seat of the little electric tourist train.

"Morning!" Kit called, pausing in wiping down the train, which already looked polished to a shine.

"Hi," Lily replied with significantly less enthusiasm.

"Are you okay?" Seren asked. "What happened to your face?"

"I had a little run in with a tree."

Kit gave a speedy shake of his head. "You did what?"

"Never mind," Lily said with a flick of her hand. "It's fine."

Seren and Kit exchanged a look.

"Is everything okay with you?" Seren asked.

"Yeah," she replied automatically, though that was pretty far from the truth. Since the police hadn't found the stolen goods at Gideon's place, she had the feeling she'd never see her backpack or its contents again.

All she could hope for now was that whoever took it had thrown the passports away without paying them any attention. She'd have to apply for a new passport, but that wasn't a huge deal.

"You look stressed," Kit said. "Is this to do with a certain police officer and his imminent departure?"

She sighed. At least the lost backpack had taken her mind off that issue. "Let's not talk about that."

"He'll be back to visit." Kit slung an arm around her shoulder and gave her a side hug, which aggravated her wounds and made her wince slightly. "And we'll be here to look after you."

"Kit!" Seren hissed from her seat on the train. "She said she doesn't want to talk about it."

"Sorry," he muttered, drawing away.

Seren slipped out of her seat to stand beside Lily. "I've heard rumours about your recent investigations."

She supposed that shouldn't be a surprise. Not much went unnoticed on St Mary's. "Unsuccessful investigations," Lily clarified. "I can't figure it out. I guess whoever was stealing stuff is going to get away with it."

"You've been keeping Len Marrack entertained anyway," Seren said. "He was in the pub last night, full of stories about how he's been helping you investigate."

Lily grimaced. "What was he saying?"

"Just that he'd been brainstorming with you about who it could be."

A low groan escaped Kit as he rolled his eyes.

"Be quiet!" Seren admonished.

"I didn't say anything!" he shot back, leaning casually against the train.

"No, but I could hear your thoughts loud and clear."

"And I'm not allowed freedom of thoughts any more?" He spluttered a laugh. "Sometimes I wonder about this whole *being in a relationship* thing."

"What are you two talking about?" Lily asked.

"Nothing," Seren said. "Ignore him."

"Since most people can't actually read my mind, she doesn't know what she's ignoring."

"Lucky her," Seren said, wrinkling her nose and exchanging a teasing look with Kit.

"You're being weird," Lily said, pushing her hair behind her ear.

"I don't like Len," Kit said out of the side of his mouth. "But apparently that's an unacceptable opinion, so I'm supposed to keep quiet."

"It's ridiculous," Seren said. "Everyone likes Len. He's like an older version of you."

"Great. I'm gonna grow up to be a pervert, am I?"

"Shut up!" Seren laughed. "He's not a pervert. He wasn't even looking at me."

Kit's twinkling eyes darted to Lily. "I came home one day to find Len staring in our kitchen window..."

"He was washing the windows," Seren said. "Because he's a window cleaner. That's his job."

"But he wasn't," Kit insisted. "He was just standing with his squeegee in his hand, peering in at you. I watched him for ages, and he just stared through the window like a creep."

"He was probably lost in a trance or something," Seren said. "There's no way he was perving on me." Her eyes flicked to Lily. "Kit told Len he thought window cleaning was a job he'd like to do for himself in the future. So if you ever wonder why our windows are filthy, now you know."

"Hey! I clean them." Kit grinned. "It's just a very tedious job."

"That's why most people pay someone to do it."

"Maybe I just don't like window cleaners in general," Kit said. "It's weird having someone looking into your house. And I don't like the way he just shows up whenever he feels like it. He should tell us when he's coming so I'm not wandering the house naked or something."

"I'll bet he sees all sorts," Seren said. "He's discreet, though. I suppose you have to be. If he went around telling stories, no one would employ him."

Lily's heart rate had steadily increased, and she had a heavy feeling in her stomach.

"You don't like him?" she asked Kit.

He shrugged. "I get dodgy vibes from him."

"Only because he has an overprotective streak," Seren put in. "If Kit thinks anyone looks at me funny, he takes issue with them."

"That's not true. Who else do I have a problem with?"

Seren opened her mouth, then closed it again with a hint of a pout.

"I don't like him," Kit said bluntly. "I'm allowed to not like people."

"But you like everyone." Lily dragged in a breath through her nose. "Seren once said if you don't like someone, it's a very bad sign..."

"Len's harmless," Seren said with slightly less conviction. "I really don't think he was looking at me."

"I don't think he was either," Lily mused.

"What?" Seren said.

Lily's gaze was fixed on the horizon. "I think he was sizing the place up." She swallowed hard. "I think he was figuring out what was worth stealing, and when would be the best time to slip inside and take whatever he had his eye on."

"Len?" Seren said. "No way."

"Oh, my god." A wave of nausea swept through Lily as she felt absolutely certain she'd been right about Len at the start. "He's played me like an absolute fiddle."

"What are you talking about?" Kit asked.

"I have to go," Lily said, then set off at a run.

Chapter Thirty-Two

Arriving at Len's house, Lily was completely out of breath. She was also confused by the two police cars parked outside.

"What's going on?" she asked when Flynn walked out of the house with a cardboard box in his arms. After depositing it beside an identical one in the boot of the closest police car, he turned to her with a triumphant glint in his eyes. "Len was the one who's been robbing people."

She swallowed hard. "How did you figure it out?"

"It occurred to me that your gut feelings about these things are usually right. So I took apart the pressure washer he was shipping off to the mainland and found a bunch of jewellery inside. I guess if we'd taken apart the vacuum cleaner the other day we'd have found something in that too."

"What else have you found?" Lily asked as the sergeant led Len out of the house with a hand on his elbow.

"Bits and pieces. Mostly jewellery, a bit of cash, a few backpacks."

Her eyes darted to the boxes. "Is this all the stolen stuff?"

Flynn nodded. "We'll take it down to the station and go through it. Hopefully, we can get everything back to the owners."

"Is my backpack in there?" she asked in a rush. "Can I have a look through and get it back?"

"*Here she is!*" Len sneered as he got close. "The island's very own investigator."

"You stole from people!" she shouted, unable to control her anger. "You stole from people who trusted you. And you lied to me. I trusted you, and you told one lie after another."

"I don't think you're one to talk about lying, are you?"

"Come on." The sergeant nudged him towards the open car door. "Don't make a fuss. You're in enough trouble as it is."

"It's her you ought to be looking into!" Len's eyes blazed. "Someone should ask Lily Larkin questions. If that's even your real name."

The sergeant hushed him and encouraged him into the car before closing the door and circling around the back to close the boot.

"Wait!" Lily said as the back door came down. "He stole my backpack. I need to get it back."

"We'll process everything and get it back to you," Sergeant Proctor said, heading for the driver's door. "You didn't report anything missing though, so you better come to the station later to make sure we've got all the paperwork straight."

"No," Lily protested, but the sergeant was already in the car.

"Don't worry," Flynn said. "You'll get it back."

"You could have just given it to me then." She glared at him. "You promised you'd get it for me."

"I will. What does it look like again?"

"It's black with a little blue flower embroidered on the front pocket."

"I think I saw that. Once we've got everything documented, I can bring it over to you."

"You can't document it," Lily said desperately. "I already told you the sergeant can't look inside it, or you. I need you to promise you won't look in it."

"Why?" He pursed his lips. "What's in it?"

"Just promise me," she snarled.

A smirk played on his lips. "What exactly is so embarrassing that you don't want me to see?"

As tears filled her eyes, she turned away from him.

"Lily," he said after a moment.

"I just need the bag back," she said, unable to hide her emotions. "I can explain everything to you later, but first I need you to get my bag... and not look inside it."

"What could be so bad?" he asked, searching her features.

"It's sentimental," she said, her voice hoarse. "Stuff I found after my uncle died. I'll show it to you later, but you can't let the sergeant see it."

"Okay." He cupped her cheek and brushed away a tear with his thumb. "I'll get it for you. Don't worry."

She squeezed his hand. "Thank you."

Flynn pulled in at the station and stepped out of the car.

"Are you okay?" he called to the sergeant, who lingered beside the Land Rover, one hand on the back panel as though steadying himself.

He nodded slowly. "Not feeling too bright. Len's wittering doesn't help."

"Do you want me to deal with him?"

Again, the sergeant nodded. "Book him in." He swiped at the glimmer of sweat on his forehead. "Since I don't think he's a danger to anyone, or a flight risk, we'll interview him and let him go on bail until he has a court date."

"Do you want me to do the interview if you're not feeling great?"

"I'll manage. I might need to go home after that, though."

"Do you need to see a doctor?" Flynn asked, concerned at the sergeant suggesting going home when there was so much to deal with. He could process the stolen goods himself, but it was unusual for the sergeant to hand over control.

"I think I'm all right," he said, moving and opening the boot. "I haven't been sleeping well. Probably just need to catch up on some shut eye."

Flynn opened the back door to let Len out, then escorted him inside and into the interview room.

The sergeant joined them a few minutes later and unbuttoned his shirt collar as he launched straight into the interview. Having been caught red-handed, Len didn't hold back, but described his crime spree over the past week, including giving the details of his contact on the mainland who he'd been selling the goods to. Mostly, he was unemotional and unremorseful.

"Why did you do it?" Flynn asked eventually.

He flexed his fingers. "My hands are shot. Arthritis. I won't be able to work for much longer, and how will I manage then?"

"So you thought you'd steal from people you've known for years?" Flynn said contemptuously.

"Me?" he scoffed. "What about *them?* They've been robbing me blind for years! They slip me cash and make out as though they're doing me a favour. What they really did was shaft me when it came to my pension."

Shaking his head, Flynn leaned back in his seat and let the sergeant take the lead again.

After a few more questions, he drew the interview to a close by charging him with burglary and theft, then left to make some phone calls.

"I bet you feel really high and mighty," Len snarled at Flynn when they were alone. "Sitting there judging me."

"If things were really so bad, you could have applied for benefits."

"Benefits wouldn't be enough to live on. Not around here."

Flynn leaned back in his chair. "So you thought you were entitled to just take what you wanted?"

"Too right. I've worked myself to the bone all these years and barely get by. The people I've cleaned for, they have it easy in their big houses. And what about your little friend? Talk about getting everything handed to you."

"What are you talking about?"

"Lily Larkin, or whatever her real name is. She leased that ice cream shop for an absolute steal. I asked about leasing it years ago and was sent on my way. That would have been a nice little earner for me, but no, it goes to some prissy rich girl. Now that was a prize – robbing her."

Flynn squinted in confusion.

"I hope you'll be asking her a few questions too," Len added.

The door opened again, and the sergeant approached the table.

"You can leave on bail," he said, sliding the papers across and informing Len of his court date in Truro the following week, as well as the consequences for not showing up. He heaved in a breath and looked at Flynn. "Make sure he understands the conditions of his bail before you let him go." He trudged to the door and left them alone again.

"Let's get this over and done with," Flynn said, taking the papers to go through everything with Len, explaining that he shouldn't go near any of the properties he'd burgled or anyone he'd stolen from. He also gave him the friendly advice to keep a low profile, since word was bound to get out that it was him who'd committed the burglaries and thefts.

With the paperwork signed, he escorted him through the station and watched him go, then he ventured back to the sergeant's office.

Sergeant Proctor was sitting at his desk. On the floor was one of the boxes of stolen goods. The other was on the desk, obscuring Flynn's view of the sergeant.

"If you need to go home, I can deal with this," he said, clocking the weariness in his superior's features.

"Do you know about this?" The sergeant's voice was oddly

aggressive as he flicked the back of his hand at the backpack on his desk.

Flynn registered the blue flower embroidered on the black material. "I think it's Lily's."

"So you knew about it?"

"She told me Len had stolen a backpack from her. I don't know the details."

"Do you know what's in it?" the sergeant asked through gritted teeth. "I'd think carefully about your answer if I were you."

"What's going on?" Flynn asked.

He pulled a bundle of clothes from the bag, then tilted it in Flynn's direction.

His eyes widened. "That's a lot of money."

"You don't know why she has so much cash?"

"No." It shed some light on Len's comments, though. Flynn thought back to how panicked Lily had been earlier. "She said the bag contained things she'd found at her uncle's house after he died."

The sergeant flicked a finger towards a couple of passports on the desk, which Flynn hadn't noticed. "Any idea why she has two passports?"

Flynn shrugged. "She grew up in different countries across Europe, so she probably has dual citizenship."

"I'd agree with you on that if it weren't for the fact that there are two different names in these passports."

"What?" He lifted the passports and opened one and then the other. "This doesn't make sense."

"Not unless she has an identical twin we don't know about, who shares neither her last name nor her nationality."

"I don't understand it," Flynn said, staring at the passports.

"You really knew nothing about it?"

He swallowed hard and shook his head.

"We need to question her."

"I can go and speak to her. I'm sure there's some simple

explanation." Though he couldn't imagine what it was. "That's why she was looking for the thief," he muttered, sinking into a chair. "She did have a vested interest in finding them. But she didn't tell me anything about it." Not only that. She'd outright lied to him.

"Flynn?" Sergeant Proctor said, interrupting his thoughts. "I think it's probably better if I question Lily."

"Maybe," he agreed. "Yeah. That might be better." He wasn't sure he could remain professional. While he was keen to know why exactly Lily had a bag full of cash and two passports, he mostly wanted to question her about why she hadn't spoken to him about it.

Whatever was going on, she should have been able to confide in him.

Chapter Thirty-Three

LILY CLOSED the shop early in the afternoon and sent Jessica home. Pacing the back room of the shop, she kept glancing through for Flynn arriving, while chewing over her plan.

She'd tell him about the money. Lots of people kept large amounts of cash without it being dodgy. Maybe her uncle had been like Silas and didn't trust banks.

There was no need to mention the passport since she planned on destroying it. Why had she even kept it to start with? All she could think of now was the relief it would bring to be rid of it. Whatever reason her uncle had for it, was nothing to do with her life now. She had a good thing going on St Mary's and she should look to the future instead of dwelling on the past.

The knock at the front door startled her, and she wandered through, her smile not disguising her confusion that it was the sergeant at the door when she was expecting Flynn.

"Hi," she said, opening the door.

"Can I come in?" His formal tone put Lily on edge, but she stepped aside and let the door fall shut behind him.

"What's going on?"

He tugged at his collar and rested a hand on the back of the nearest chair. "I need you to explain the contents of the backpack Len Marrack stole from you."

Her stomach turned to stone. "My backpack?" she said weakly.

"Yes. The one you neglected to report stolen and which contains large sums of cash and two passports... one of which I assume is a forgery."

Lily's jaw hung open.

"You can start by explaining the passports," the sergeant said.

"I... umm..." Her heart beat so hard that her blood pulsated uncomfortably through her veins.

"You're not denying that you have two passports with two different names?"

Swallowing hard, she pulled her shoulders back. "No."

"Lily." He rubbed at his forehead and sighed heavily. "What on earth is going on?"

"It's hard to explain, but..."

"But what?"

"I think maybe I need a lawyer."

The look he gave her was mostly disappointment. "If you think you need a lawyer, you probably do. I'll need you to come down to the station for a formal interview. If you don't have a lawyer, I can arrange one for you."

Tears threatened behind Lily's eyes, but she blinked them away. "Now?" she asked.

"Yes, now."

She glanced behind her. "I need to run upstairs and lock up."

"Go on then," he said and sank onto the nearest chair.

As she ascended the stairs to the flat, Lily pulled her phone from her pocket and took a deep breath. She had no idea if Maria knew more about her childhood than she'd let on, but now seemed like as good a time as any to ask her outright.

At the door to the flat she tapped away, telling Maria about the money and the passports and the fact that the sergeant was taking her to the police station.

If you know anything at all, she typed at the end of the message. *Please help me.*

She hit send without stopping to think or reread the message. Then she locked up the flat and went back downstairs.

"Are you okay?" she asked Sergeant Proctor as he stood with what appeared to be a fair amount of effort.

"Fine. Let's get to the station and get this over and done with."

They walked in silence to the police station. The vague sense of fear in the depths of her stomach was replaced by annoyance when she clapped eyes on Flynn sitting at the front desk. He'd promised he'd get her the backpack without anyone looking in it. She'd trusted him to do that, but he clearly hadn't trusted her enough to not look.

"We should let Len go on bail," the sergeant said. "On the condition that he doesn't approach anyone he stole from. In fact, he probably shouldn't leave his house."

Flynn stood slowly, his eyebrows lifted. "He's already gone. We sent him home before you left to speak with Lily."

"Oh, yeah." He rubbed the back of his neck. "Lily has agreed to a voluntary interview."

"Are you feeling okay?" Flynn asked, coming around the desk to the sergeant.

"I'm fine." He stood up straighter. "I'm just going to get a breath of fresh air, then I'll interview Lily."

The room was eerily quiet as he pushed at the door and walked outside.

"He seems a little under the weather," Lily remarked.

"It's been a long day." Flynn worried at his bottom lip. "What's going on?"

"I wish I knew," she said sadly.

"Why do you have two passports?"

"I honestly don't know," she said, desperate for him to believe her. "I found the money and passport after my uncle died."

"Why did you keep it?"

Her shoulders slumped. "I've been asking myself the same question for days. Part of me wanted to know why he had it. I had hoped Maria might have some clues for me, but she doesn't seem to know any more than I do." She scrubbed a hand down her face. "How much trouble am I in?"

"Depends. If the money was obtained legally and if the forged passport was never used, then things will be slightly better."

"I've never used it. I've never travelled on it or anything. At least not as far as I know. I swear I only knew about it when Uncle Derek died."

Flynn looked at her sadly. "Even having a forged passport in your possession could get you ten years in prison."

"You can't be serious?" Her heart pounded even more furiously. She felt dizzy, and slightly nauseous. "I can't go to prison. I didn't do anything."

"Are you telling me the truth?"

"Yes." She hated that he had to ask, and was about to comment on that when the walkie talkie on his desk let out a shrill tone that was impossible to ignore. "What's that?" she asked as he set off to the desk.

"Someone's pressed the red button."

"What does that mean?"

"Either an officer is in trouble and needs immediate backup, or they pressed the button by accident." He lifted the radio and muttered a curse as he looked at the display.

"What's wrong?" Lily asked.

"Wait here," he said, running for the door. "Just stay here. I'll be back."

Stunned, Lily stared at the door for a minute. Then she sank onto a chair to await her fate.

Chapter Thirty-Four

Flynn was vaguely aware of how hard his boots hit the pavement as he ran full pelt down the road. His eyes were fixed on the shape of the sergeant, sitting slumped against a wall.

At the speed Flynn ran, it was a struggle to stop when he reached him.

"Sarge!" he called out, dropping in front of him. "Graham, can you hear me?"

The sergeant's hand, which had been loosely clutching his walkie talkie, fell away as Flynn felt for a pulse.

Swiftly, he moved him onto his back. Both of their radios emitted chatter from the control room.

Flynn pressed the button on his own walkie talkie. "This is PC Grainger. I've found Sergeant Proctor. He's unresponsive. I suspect a cardiac arrest. Send an ambulance immediately. I'm starting CPR now."

With the message received, he mentally blocked out further response from the control room and focused on counting chest compressions.

Chapter Thirty-Five

After five minutes of sitting in the eerily quiet police station, the sound of sirens had Lily venturing to the door and peering out at the street. With nothing to see, she was about to retreat inside when a figure caught her eye.

"Maria!" she called as the woman hurried towards her.

"I came as soon as I got your message."

"Thanks. Did you hear sirens?"

She nodded. "There were flashing lights at the end of the road, but I came from the other direction. What's going on? Have you been arrested?"

"No. The sergeant just wants to interview me for now. But he left, and then Flynn got some emergency call and ran off. I'm supposed to stay here... I don't know what's going on."

Maria ushered her back inside. "Tell me about the money and the passports," she said as they sat side by side on the bench seat that ran along the wall.

"I found it when Uncle Derek died. He had a bunch of cash. Lots of it. And forged passports for both of us. I got rid of his. I'm not sure why I kept mine. Part of me wondered if I might need it... he must have had it for a reason. But I really wish I hadn't held onto it. According to Flynn, I could be looking at a decade in prison."

"Surely not," Maria said. "Not when you didn't know anything about it. Once you explain you had nothing to do with it – that you just found it in your uncle's things – everything will be fine."

"That might be true if Uncle Derek were around to verify my story and explain that there was nothing illegal going on. But I have no proof that I didn't acquire it myself and that I wasn't planning something nefarious."

Maria rubbed at her forehead. "What a mess."

"Why did he have fake passports?" Lily asked desperately. "Was he some kind of spy?"

"No." She huffed out a laugh. "Nothing like that."

Lily sat ramrod straight. "You know why he had them then?"

"Yes."

"You've been keeping secrets from me this whole time?"

"I didn't know how much you knew," she protested. "I didn't want to raise old issues that would upset you for no reason."

"Can you please tell me now, since whatever you know might be the only thing that stops me from spending the next decade behind bars."

"I'm sure that won't happen."

"Please tell me whatever you know... the sergeant and Flynn will be back any minute."

She squeezed her eyes closed. "It'll sound insane."

"My life feels pretty insane at this moment, anyway."

She exhaled a long breath. "Derek was never convinced your parents' deaths were an accident."

"He thought someone started the fire at our house on purpose?" Lily whispered.

Maria nodded. "That was only the start of it."

"The fire at the ice cream shop?"

"Yes. But that was a little later..."

"How do you mean?"

"Derek had been asking questions. The fire at your parents' house was deemed accidental. Faulty electrics or something. No one's fault, or so they said. But Derek had his suspicions, and so did your grandma."

"My grandparents all died either before I was born or when I was tiny. I never knew any of them."

"You knew Clara. Maybe you don't remember her, but she was a big part of your life when you were little."

A lump swelled in Lily's throat. "Did you know her?"

"No. But Derek talked about her a lot. She sounded like a force to be reckoned with."

"She was my mum's mum?" Lily asked.

"Yes." She pressed her lips together. "I don't know if you remember, but the house you lived in with your parents was on a cul-de-sac. Right at the edge of the town. Your mum had grown up in the house and was attached to it. Property developers wanted to buy out all the houses on the street, but your parents refused to sell. As far as I understand it, there were some aggressive conversations with the company that wanted to buy... and then your house burned down. Derek and Clara didn't think it was a coincidence."

"But they didn't find any evidence?"

"No. And it seemed that someone didn't like them digging into it."

Lily shook her head. "What happened?"

"Your grandma got a couple of threatening notes. Then she was walking home from the shops one evening when she had a nasty fall down stone steps. It didn't kill her outright, but she was in bad shape. I don't think she was conscious much, but she came around for long enough to tell Derek that someone had pushed her. And that he needed to stop looking into your parents' deaths and focus on keeping you safe. She told him to take you and get away from Truro."

"And he did," Lily murmured.

"I don't think he was fully convinced that running was the answer. He brought you over to visit me again."

"That's when the fire happened at the ice cream shop?"

"Yes." She nodded sadly. "It didn't seem as though the intention was to harm anyone, more that someone was sending a message."

"Why did no one know I was here? I asked Glynis and Mirren – neither of them remembered you having guests."

"Derek didn't want anyone to know. After the incident with your gran, he got paranoid. He'd barely let you out of his sight. When the smoke alarms went off that night, he bundled you and your things together and slipped out through the back door."

"I vaguely remember," Lily said.

"You slept in his arms on the beach that night, and he left with you the next day."

It took a few minutes for Lily to trust herself to speak through the emotions, which felt as though they might suffocate her. "We always used our real names, didn't we? Why did he have fake passports?"

"He got them later. About a year after you moved to Italy, he caught some private investigator watching you at the school gates. I believe he beat the guy up, then he moved you to Spain. He found someone dealing in fake passports and got them as a security measure. He was trying his best to keep things relatively normal for you, so he didn't want to change your names and identities. But he also wanted to be ready in case that became necessary."

"You were right," Lily said, her voice brittle. "This all sounds insane."

"I'm sorry."

"Will you tell the police all of this?" Lily blinked away tears. "I'm not sure anyone will believe I have a forged passport, but don't know why."

"Of course. I'll help however I can."

Lily's gaze flicked to the door. "I don't know what's going on. Where did they go?" She pulled out her phone and messaged Flynn, but got no reply.

"Where are you?" she murmured, eyes not shifting from the door.

Chapter Thirty-Six

His radio had gone quiet, but Flynn was aware of his colleagues at the other end, waiting for an update. The ones whose voices had been there in the background while he'd administered CPR and while he'd sat in the back of the ambulance, watching the paramedic attempting to shock the sergeant's heart back into rhythm.

It didn't look good. That was what he'd told his colleagues on the mainland when the sergeant was wheeled into the hospital amid a bustle of hospital personnel.

He hung back in the waiting area, head bent, staring at his hands, which trembled slightly as the adrenaline subsided.

An occasional glance at the clock told him it was almost half an hour before the doctor finally came out to him.

"Sorry," she murmured, eyes glassy with tears.

Flynn took a sudden interest in his boots. They could do with a polish. He'd do that later.

"You did everything you could," Dr Redwood said, sinking onto the chair beside him.

"That's probably not true."

"It is true." She put a hand on his shoulder. "He was gone when you got to him. No one could have done anything."

"What about this morning when he complained of feeling dizzy?" His throat squeezed painfully around the words. "I probably could have done something then. Or yesterday when he was looking really pale. Or the entire week when he's been saying he was tired and not feeling great."

She rubbed gently on his shoulder blade. "It's always the same with something like this. The signs are there, but they can easily be dismissed as something else, or nothing at all. Even I would have told him he just needed a holiday or a couple of days of rest."

"I doubt it. You'd have checked him out properly and seen there was a problem with his heart."

"Don't beat yourself up," she whispered. "You really couldn't have done anything to prevent this."

Flynn's chest tightened, and a lone teardrop splashed onto his boot.

"The two of you were pretty close, weren't you?" Dr Redwood said.

"Yeah," he managed. "We got on well."

"Someone needs to tell his wife. Where's PC Hill?"

"He's been on holiday for a week. He heard about the sergeant from control and messaged me to say he was on his way to the airport. I need to update him." His fingers went to his radio. "I need to update them all."

"I can speak to his wife, but I think it will be better coming from you, since you were with him."

His throat clogged again at the thought of that grim task. "Maybe I should wait for PC Hill. He knows her better."

"Don't risk her hearing from someone else," Dr Redwood said kindly. "Besides, you'll be able to relate to her better."

"How so?"

"She'll probably blame herself too."

He nodded once but couldn't quite bring himself to move. "We just let Len Marrack out on bail for burglary," he said, then attempted to make a mental list of what needed to be done. He heaved in a breath as he thought about Lily waiting at the station. "I have to interview someone at the station. And I don't know what happens now... I guess PC Hill will be acting sergeant until they find a replacement. There's so much to do."

"You can manage it. Just deal with it how the sergeant would. But first, you need to speak to his wife."

He sucked in a breath and attempted to pull himself together. "I need to nip back to the station. Then I'll go and speak to her."

After thanking the doctor, he walked outside in a daze.

He could do this, he told himself as he focused on putting one foot in front of the other.

He was fairly sure he wasn't about to deal with things the way the sergeant would. But he hoped the sergeant would understand his actions regarding Lily.

He was fairly sure he wouldn't be surprised by them.

Chapter Thirty-Seven

As the minutes ticked by, Lily had the increasing notion that something wasn't right. What could have kept Flynn and the sergeant away for so long?

"Flynn's leaving next week," she said, breaking the silence.

Maria nodded. "I heard. Glynis is worried it'll be hard for you."

That felt like a massive understatement. "I keep thinking something will happen and he won't have to leave, but there's only a week to go, so I'm not sure how much longer I can keep my head in the sand."

"Are you and him together?"

Slowly, Lily nodded. "He thinks we can have a long-distance relationship, but I'm not sure they ever work out."

"I expect it'll be tough, but if you love each other, you'll make it work."

"Did you love Derek?" Lily asked, not disguising the hint of bitterness in her words.

"Yes," Maria said quietly.

"Do you think he loved you?"

"I like to think so."

"That disproves your theory then."

She was saved from the awkward atmosphere by the door opening. At the sight of Flynn, she shot out of her seat.

"Where did you go?"

"There was an emergency," he said, a faraway look in his eyes. "Sorry it took so long."

"It's probably a good thing anyway," she blurted out. "Because Maria is here now, and she knows about the passport. It's a wild story, but I think I know how you can verify it..." She talked rapidly, telling him about her uncle's theory that someone had killed her parents and grandmother, and had been coming after her too. She could hear how unbelievable it all sounded, but Flynn barely reacted to any of it – just stared at her blankly as she rushed through it all.

"I'm sure if you look back through the files about my parents' death there'll be something about my uncle and grandma asking questions. And my grandma probably told the police she thought someone pushed her. I'd think so anyway." Finally, she stopped talking.

"Why did he have so much cash?" Flynn asked.

Lily opened her mouth to say she didn't know, but Maria answered for her.

"If he needed to hide, he knew anyone could track them down through the bank. He wanted to always have enough so that they could rely on that and be untraceable."

"Makes sense," he said. "So it was legally obtained?"

"Yes. Derek had plenty of money – from Lily's parents and from her grandmother. They lived off that, and he withdrew his wages from the bank every month. That way, if anyone ever questioned it, he had proof of where it came from. He'd just look like a man who didn't trust banks."

Flynn nodded and moved towards the back rooms. "Wait here a second," he said without looking at them.

Lily frowned at how odd his voice sounded. Hollow almost.

"That was weird," Maria said. "It almost seemed as though he didn't even care."

Lily whipped around to the front door. "Why is he alone?" she said, thinking aloud.

She barely had time to ponder it before Flynn reappeared.

"What was the emergency?" she asked.

Ignoring the question, he held out her backpack. "Get rid of the passport," he said in that same dull monotone. "If you're sure the money is legal, you should probably start spending it. The pounds anyway. You'll have to get the euros changed or you could deposit them into the bank ... but don't make any big transactions."

"I don't understand what's going on," she said, taking the bag when he thrust it at her. "Where's Sergeant Proctor?"

Flynn swallowed hard. "He had a heart attack."

Lily sucked in a sharp breath. "Is he okay?"

The slight shake of Flynn's head made no sense.

"No one else knows about your backpack," he went on. "Except for Len, but if I deny any knowledge of it, no one will believe a word he says. As long as you get rid of the passport, there's no proof to back up what he says. Maybe hide the cash for now, just in case. Not at your place. Somewhere else."

"Flynn?" Lily blinked back tears. "The sergeant?"

"He died." His chin quivered before he pulled his shoulders back. "I need to go and tell his wife, so you have to leave."

"He died?" *That can't be right.* "He can't be dead."

"He had a heart attack," Flynn repeated, then pressed his lips together. "I did CPR, but..." He trailed off with another shake of his head.

Lily felt rooted to the spot. "I'm so sorry, Flynn."

"I have a lot to do," he said robotically. "Please, just go. I'll call you later."

When she took a step towards him, he took one back. "I have things that I have to do. I need to talk to his wife... I'll call you later, but... I can't do this now. I just need to get things done."

"Yeah. Of course." She bit down on her lip and nodded her understanding. He couldn't deal with sympathy. He had to keep it together and get through his tasks. As much as it might feel like rejection, it wasn't about her. "Call me if you need anything," she said and gave him what she hoped was a comforting smile before she walked outside with Maria.

Without discussion, they set off back to the ice cream shop, neither of them speaking until they were inside with the door locked behind them.

"Poor Flynn," Maria said. "He seemed really shaken up."

"He and the sergeant had got pretty close." Lily sank onto the nearest chair. "He was a nice man. I can't believe he's dead. How can he be dead?"

Of course, there was no answer to that, and they sat in stunned silence for a few minutes.

Eventually, Lily loosened her grip on the backpack and set it by her feet. Opening the top, she withdrew the passports and everything else except the money. "Could you do me a favour and keep hold of this until I know Len won't make a fuss about it?"

"Of course." Maria picked up the bag. "I promise I won't touch any of it."

"I'm not worried about that. You can spend the lot as far as I'm concerned."

"I'll just keep it safe."

"Thank you. For everything."

She chewed her lip. "I didn't do anything."

"I'll probably have more questions," Lily said. "I can't think straight now, but I guess I'll think of things later."

"I don't know if there's much more I can tell you, but I'll do my best to answer any questions you have."

Lily walked Maria to the door. "It feels a little odd to finally have answers. Especially as I was starting to think I'd never know the truth about my childhood."

"I can't imagine knowing is much of a relief, given what you've found."

"It's better than not knowing. I really wondered whether Uncle Derek was some kind of spy."

"I think he'd probably have liked that notion."

"Probably."

Maria stepped outside, then turned back. "Call me if you need anything."

After thanking her again, Lily watched her walk away, eyes on the backpack, which had felt like such a burden over the last ten months. Sharing her problems definitely made the burden easier to bear.

Trudging upstairs, she shot off a message to Flynn, then stood over the sink and watched her forged passport go up in flames.

The relief was immediate, but her mind soon wandered to the events of the day. She thought about Flynn having to tell the sergeant's wife that her husband was dead. Her chest squeezed at the thought, and tears filled her eyes as she ran through a snapshot reel of her time getting to know the sergeant over the last five months.

When the waves of grief passed, she mostly felt numb. And also a little guilty.

Because as sad as she was about the sergeant, she couldn't help but wonder if this meant that Flynn might be able to keep his job on St Mary's.

Chapter Thirty-Eight

Lily fell asleep waiting to hear from Flynn. The next morning she found a message had come through after midnight, saying it had been a long day and he was heading home for some sleep. He said he'd speak to her tomorrow.

Opening the shop felt somehow disrespectful, in the way that getting on with life feels wrong when someone has died.

After her uncle had died, Lily had felt an overwhelming urge to shout at random people for continuing their everyday activities as though nothing had happened.

Now she was one of those people – just getting on with life. The mood was fairly sombre in the shop, with a lot of locals coming in merely to exchange a few words and comment on how sad it was. Lily agreed on repeat. She was growing weary of having the same conversation when the woman who worked at the post office came in late in the morning.

"It must be awful for you," she remarked after the standard mournful words.

Lily's head darted up. "How do you mean?"

"I assume you were one of the last people to see him."

"When?" Lily asked, her heart rate skyrocketing.

"I saw you walking through town with him yesterday afternoon. That can't have been long before he died."

"Oh." Her thoughts felt jumbled, like a tangled ball of wool. "Yes. I'd been investigating the thefts, and he had a few questions for me." She sounded defensive. She *was* defensive.

"That's terrible as well. Len's been cleaning my windows for years. It's coming to something, isn't it, when you can't even trust the window cleaner? Thankfully, I have nothing worth stealing. The perks of being poor, I suppose."

Lily frowned at the woman who irritated her even on a good day. Today, she had no patience with her at all. "Did you want an ice cream?"

"No. Just stretching my legs on my break. Take care of yourself," she said as she left.

"You can go home," Lily called to Jessica, who was wiping down a table she was certain didn't need wiping.

"Are you sure?"

"Yes. I can't think it's going to be busy this afternoon. And I'll probably close early. It feels weird to carry on as normal."

"I suppose keeping busy is better than sitting around being sad." Jessica wrung out her cloth and hung it over the tap. She fetched her bag and denim jacket, but lingered by the counter before coming over and giving Lily a big hug.

"It's probably not a good time to mention it, but Rhys wants to book flights to the mainland. He wants to go in the middle of September, but I said I'd need to check with you. I can tell him we'll go at the end of September instead if it's better for you."

Lily could hardly look at her, and ran her gaze over the ice cream instead. "It's fine," she said. "I already told you to do what's best for you. Just let me know when you've booked it."

"I will," she said quietly, then told Lily to have a good afternoon.

"Thanks," she replied, fairly sure there'd be nothing remotely good about it.

It was after eleven in the evening when Flynn arrived at Lily's door.

"How are you?" she asked, though the answer was obvious from his face. Sad and worn out, and barely holding it together. "Have you eaten?" She reached for his hand. "I made food in case you turned up hungry at some point. I can heat it up."

"I don't know when I ate," he said. "But I'm not hungry."

"I'll warm up some chicken pie. Maybe you'll feel like eating when it's in front of you."

He followed her into the kitchen and sat slumped at the table. "I probably should have gone home for a shower at least, but..." He paused, scrubbed a hand over his face. "I just wanted to come here," he said eventually.

"How's it been at work?" she asked once she'd pressed start on the microwave.

"Busy. So much paperwork and so many phone calls."

Nodding, she moved beside him, running her hand through his hair as he rested his head against her hip. They stayed that way until the microwave dinged.

He managed a few mouthfuls of chicken but mostly just pushed the food around the plate.

"I got rid of the fake passport," Lily said eventually.

"That's good."

"Did Len say anything about it?"

"Not since I interviewed him yesterday, but I didn't know what he was talking about. If he brings it up again, I'll play dumb. I've already made it clear that it was your theory about him sneaking stolen goods onto the ferry that got him caught, so it'll look as though he has a grudge against you. No one will give any credit to his claims."

"Thank you," she said with weight.

He shrugged and pushed his plate away. "Do you mind if I jump in the shower?"

"Help yourself."

He stood. "And is it okay if I sleep here?"

"Of course."

Emerging from the shower in his boxers and a T-shirt, he slung his uniform over the chair in Lily's room and sat beside her on the bed.

"I know you have a lot going on at the moment," Lily said, "but if you're angry with me about the backpack, you should just say so."

The sorrow in his eyes had her cursing herself for bringing it up and adding to his stress.

"I'm upset that you didn't tell me about it sooner. I assume you spent all week trying to track down your bag, and lying to me."

"I didn't want to put you in an awkward position. You're a police officer, and I knew you'd have to report it."

"I wouldn't have reported it," he said blandly. "I'd have helped you get it back."

"It wouldn't have been that straightforward for you," she argued.

"Yes, it would." He turned to face her. "Maybe it shouldn't be that straightforward, but it would have been. I'd have helped you."

"Not if it meant ignoring the law."

"Yes," he said firmly. "I would have ignored the law, or even broken the law. I don't care. You'll always come first. I would break the law for you every day of the week if I had to."

Tears filled Lily's eyes as she ran her hand down his cheek.

His mouth twitched into a shadow of a smile. "Please don't test me on that. I'd rather not break the law."

Since she couldn't find any appropriate words, she leaned close enough to feel his breath on her mouth, then kissed him softly.

In response, he took her face in his hands and devoured her lips with his.

Chapter Thirty-Nine

Lily tried to let Flynn sleep, but his arm was draped across a particularly bruised part of her hip, and her attempt at deep breathing wasn't dulling the pain of it.

"Sorry," he muttered when she removed his arm. "Was I hurting you?"

"It's okay," she insisted. "Your hand was pressing on a bruise, but it's fine."

"Let me check..." When he lifted the covers, the cool air made goosebumps erupt over her naked skin.

"Flynn!" She pulled the duvet back over herself.

"You look good to me," he said playfully.

She raised her head for him to slip his arm under and then settled herself at his collarbone. "I wish we could just stay in bed all day."

"Me too." His previous relaxed state vanished as he turned his wrist to check his watch. "I should get to the station."

"Could you maybe spare half an hour?" she asked with her best flirty smile. Surely he could give her a quick repeat of last night's activities before he left.

"I wish," he said. "I need to shower and get to work. Hopefully, I won't be too late tonight though."

"Okay," she said, ignoring the disappointment and focusing on the view of his naked backside as he headed for the shower.

While he got ready for work, she moved to the kitchen and made a pot of coffee.

"I need to ask you something?" she said, handing him a mug when he joined her.

"Go on."

She sipped her coffee, searching for the right words. "I was wondering what happens now about your job."

"How do you mean?"

She twisted her lips to one side. "I know this sounds insensitive, but there's a job opening now, isn't there? Can you stay?"

He stared at her for one long moment. "There's an opening for a sergeant. I'm not a sergeant."

"I know you said you didn't want to be a sergeant, but you also said in theory you could."

"One day. But not now. I'm not qualified to be a sergeant. I'd have to take exams. There's a whole process."

"What about PC Hill? Can't he take the sergeant job and you take his job?"

"No," he said impatiently.

"Why not?"

"Because PC Hill doesn't want to be a sergeant." He set his mug down heavily. "There's a new sergeant arriving on Wednesday."

It took her a moment to remember what day it was. *Monday.* "That's fast."

"Yeah."

"So you're still leaving?"

He nodded.

"On Saturday?"

"I've changed the flight to Monday. There'll be a memorial service for the sergeant on Sunday, and I want to be here for that, but as of Friday I officially don't work here any more. I'm down for a shift in London next Thursday."

She felt sick. "Next Thursday?"

He nodded again.

"So, a week from now you'll be back in London?"

"I have tried to speak to you about this," he said. "You never wanted to discuss it."

"No, I didn't." She still didn't. "I kept hoping something would change, and you'd be able to stay." She watched him intently as he reached for his coffee again. The nausea she'd previously felt was replaced by fiery anger. "Would you have stayed if it had been a possibility?"

His features scrunched up. "What?"

"Sometimes, it feels as though you want to go. You're so calm about it – as though it's fine with you."

With a frustrated growl, he paced the small room. "I don't want to go. If I had a choice, of course I'd stay. But I've never had a choice."

"You do have a choice," she snapped. "You could just stay."

"Without a job?"

She nodded while her windpipe constricted. "Stay here with me."

"You know I can't," he said sadly.

Tears filled her eyes and dripped down her cheeks. "I know, but I thought I'd ask anyway ... because I really don't think long-distance relationships work."

"Ours will." He stared into his coffee. "And it's only temporary, anyway."

"Do you really think a job will magically become available here?"

"Not *magically,* no! But Sergeant Proctor did a lot of groundwork. I really think eventually it will be deemed necessary to have another officer here. And when that decision is made, I'll be first in line for the job."

"I think you're being naïve," she said fiercely. "I know what will happen. You're all fired up now, but once you get back to London, you'll forget about your life here."

He inhaled a deep breath. Opening his mouth, he started to speak, then clamped his mouth shut again as his eyes sparked with irritation.

When he walked out of the kitchen, she expected to hear the front door close behind him, but as far as she could tell he didn't leave the flat. After five minutes of silence, she wandered to the living room and found him on the couch with his head in his hands.

"There is another option," he said, turning his head in her direction. "You could come to London with me."

Her tear ducts sprang into action again. "I can't..."

"Not forever," he said calmly. "Just until I get a job here again, then we'll come back together."

"If I come to London with you, it will end up being permanent."

He shook his head. "I really think I can get my job back here. We just need to be patient."

For a moment, she actually considered going to London. But then she glanced out of the window at the stretch of golden sand and the stunning expanse of sea, which had looked dark and brooding yesterday, but was enticingly turquoise today. Seagulls squawked as they sailed on the wind. She thought of the ice cream machines, and all she'd learned about making ice cream. Her mind conjured the chatter and laughter in the shop while people indulged in the treats she'd made.

For the first time in her life, she had a job that she loved, and she had friends...

"This is my home," she said, as she sat beside Flynn.

"We'd come back." He wiped tears from her cheeks. "I promise you."

"There's nothing for me in London. You'd be working long hours, and I'd be twiddling my thumbs."

"You could find a job."

"I have a job here." She nudged his hand from her face and drew away. "I don't want to leave. You won't stay. Maybe that should tell us everything we need to know about where this relationship is headed. Neither of us will put the relationship above our jobs." She lifted her shoulders in a shrug. "If I go with you, I'll end up resenting you, the same as you'd resent me if you stayed here without a job."

"But I'm not choosing my job over you," he said. "I'm only trying to find a temporary solution while we figure things out."

"I think we need to be realistic," she said. "A long-distance relationship will only drag things out. We'll just end up arguing on the phone until we can't even be bothered to call each other any more."

"That's not true."

"A clean break will be easier in the long run," she said, wondering if they were her own words or her uncle's. She was fairly sure he'd drummed them into her whenever they moved to a new city and she'd been desperate to stay in touch with her friends. "It might be for the best," she whispered.

He stayed quiet for so long she thought she might have convinced him.

"I have to go to work," he said eventually. "But I can tell you now that if you want a clean break from me... you're going to be sorely disappointed. You might give up on us because things get hard, but I won't."

More tears spilled down her cheeks, and she tasted the salt of them as they ran over her lips. "I just don't want you to leave," she said.

Shifting in front of her, he kissed her softly. "We'll figure this out. I promise."

The sureness of his voice might have convinced her. Except she genuinely couldn't see how their relationship would survive them living hundreds of miles apart.

Chapter Forty

After a few hectic days, things settled down at the Isles of Scilly police station. Flynn spent most of Monday morning catching up on comments on their social media pages. In contrast with his previous feelings about that task, it felt pretty therapeutic now – especially given that most of the people posting were familiar to him after six months on the islands.

If the social media page was all he had to deal with, then life was as it should be on St Mary's. He was sure Sergeant Proctor would agree.

Late in the afternoon, he picked up his phone to message Lily, then hesitated. He'd go and see her instead. The atmosphere between them that morning had been tense, and he suspected he could have handled it better. Somehow, he needed to reassure her that his move was only temporary.

Walking into the back rooms, he found PC Hill packing things into a box in Sergeant Proctor's office.

"I thought the sergeant's wife wanted to come and sort through his belongings."

"She did," Jeff said. "But she called me earlier and said she couldn't face coming down here. Asked me to do it."

"You should have said. I can help."

Gently, he laid a photo of the sergeant and his wife in the box. "Thanks, but I'm almost done. It's not that much, really."

"Are you okay?" Flynn asked when his colleague sank heavily into the chair behind the desk.

"I feel as though I made a massive mistake."

"How do you mean?"

Jeff blew out a breath. "I should have taken the sergeant's job. Then you could've stayed on. It would've been you and me, and everything would have been all right. Now, I'm stuck with a new sergeant who I'm not convinced I'm going to like. Not given the phone call I had with him earlier."

"Why, what did he say?"

He shrugged. "Nothing terrible – he just seemed a little insensitive about the whole situation. Honestly, I didn't think it would all go so fast. I thought I'd be acting sergeant for a few weeks at least, and you'd be able to stay on for a while to ease the transition."

"It does all feel a bit rushed," Flynn agreed. "How did they find a new sergeant so quickly?"

Jeff curled his lip. "I think he's been waiting for a sergeant's position for ages, and has been turned down for lots of jobs."

"Not a great sign," Flynn said.

"No," Jeff agreed. "If I'd known how things would turn out, I'd have thought harder about taking the sergeant's job myself."

"You said you didn't want to be a sergeant."

"I didn't. I *don't*. Once upon a time, I had a girlfriend who thought I should be more ambitious, so I took all the exams and everything, but when it came to it, I'm happy being a constable. I don't want the extra responsibility."

Flynn nodded. "I think I'm the same. Promotions aren't on my list of priorities."

"I don't think I'd be a good sergeant. Stick to your strengths, I reckon."

"Yeah," Flynn said, though he wished Jeff had stepped into the sergeant's role. "I can't believe this is my last week."

"Me neither." He sat up straighter. "You know Sergeant Proctor was stirring things up – making a fuss about needing an extra officer on the islands. Maybe that will happen still."

"I'm hoping so," Flynn said. "But it won't happen before the weekend."

Jeff leaned back in his chair and dragged his hands through his hair. "I hate all of this. I keep expecting Graham to walk in the door, or to wake up and find this has all been a bad dream."

"Same," Flynn said, glancing around the room. "Are you sure you don't need any help in here?"

Jeff shook his head. "By the way, I had word from forensics about that necklace you found at Gideon Rowe's place."

"And?"

"It's clean. They couldn't find fingerprints or any other fibres."

"Not a massive surprise."

"No. I'm wondering whether to question Len Marrack again. See if we can get him to confess to planting it there."

"It's up to you," Flynn said, hoping he sounded casual. "He claimed he didn't know anything about it when we interviewed him. To be honest, I'm not sure it's worth pressing him about it. I guess he just threw it inside when he was supposed to be cleaning windows."

"And then he gave you an anonymous tip to search the place?" Jeff asked, tilting his head.

"Yeah." He swallowed hard. "We had a call from an unknown number saying we should search there. I imagine it was him. He just wanted to keep us off track while he got the stolen goods off the islands."

"It almost worked," Jeff said.

"Yeah." Flynn backed up to the door, keen to put an end to the conversation. "I might go out for a wander if you don't need me for anything here."

"Fine by me," Jeff said, then got back to placing items in the box.

Outside, the sunlight was dazzling, and the sky was a cheerful shade of royal blue. "Finally," Flynn muttered. After all the drizzle and grey skies for the last couple of weeks, the sunshine was a welcome sight.

It did, however, mean there was a queue in the ice cream shop and a lot of bustle outside it too. Loitering outside, he watched Lily handing out ice creams with Jessica at her side.

"Is she okay?" a voice asked beside him.

"Hi," he said to Maria, then shrugged in reply to the question. "I'd say she's been better. She was pretty stressed out this morning."

"You can hardly blame her. The poor thing has a lot on her plate."

Flynn gave a curt nod.

"I heard you're going back to London soon."

"Yes. Just until I can figure out a way to get a job here again. Lily won't believe that it's just temporary."

"That makes sense." She inclined her head, and they walked towards the beach. "From what I know, she grew up without much stability. Finally, she feels settled here, and now the rug is being pulled out from under her. You're leaving, and Jessica is leaving. I think she'd grown pretty fond of Sergeant Proctor so that must be a blow too. And if all that isn't hard enough, I've just told her that her parents may have been murdered. Her grandmother too."

Flynn lifted his eyebrows. He'd been so caught up with his own problems, he'd barely stopped to think about everything that Lily was dealing with. He definitely could have been more patient with her.

"It's surprising she's managing as well as she is," he said, wishing he didn't have to leave next week. "Will you keep an eye on her?" he asked. "When I'm not here."

"Yes. I came to see how she was doing, but I'll come back when she's not so busy." She took a step away. "If I don't see you before you leave, take care of yourself. And come back soon."

"I intend to," he said and returned her smile before she wandered away.

A moment later, Maria glanced back over her shoulder. "And make the most of this sunshine," she said cheerfully.

"Yeah." He turned to watch the families enjoying the beach, then smiled to himself as an idea came to him.

Chapter Forty-One

A MID-MORNING VISIT from Seren and Kit lifted Lily's spirits, as did the beautiful weather and the buzz of the busy shop. The lack of contact from Flynn bothered her, and she regretted how grumpy she'd been with him that morning. Not that she had much time to dwell on it given the constant stream of customers in the afternoon. When she spotted him loitering outside, she felt immediately better.

At least until she arrived back from the back room and there was no sign of him.

"Did Flynn come in?" she asked Jessica.

"I haven't seen him," she said while scooping chocolate ice cream. "Why?"

"I thought I saw him outside." She wandered to the door and looked along the promenade, but there was no sign of him. She lingered for a few minutes, basking in the warm sun on her face and enjoying the sight of families on the beach.

"Did you find him?" Jessica asked when she went back inside.

"No." She already had her phone out and fired off a quick message: *sorry about this morning*.

He replied immediately. *Don't worry about it. I finish work in a couple of hours. I'll come over then.*

She responded with a smiley face.

"Everything okay?" Jessica asked after handing over change to an elderly lady.

"Fine." Lily glanced outside at the gorgeous blue sky. "Do you think you can manage alone for the rest of the day?"

"Yeah. Of course." The flash of delight in Jessica's eyes made it very clear she enjoyed looking after the place on her own.

After a trip to the supermarket, Lily got to work cooking.

When Flynn arrived two hours later, he looked into the flat with a frown. "Did you cook?" he asked, following her into the kitchen.

"I made sausage rolls," she told him, "and a quiche and cheese pastries. All from scratch." She turned back to him. "I thought it was about time we had our picnic."

His lips twitched into a playful smile. "Great minds think alike," he said, dropping his backpack from his shoulder.

"You made a picnic too?" she asked as his arms encircled her waist.

"Yes." He dropped his forehead to hers. "I told you we'd get some decent weather eventually."

With her hands on his neck, she looked him in the eyes. "I wanted to do something nice after I was so grumpy with you this morning."

"It doesn't matter," he said quickly. "But I do want to talk to you about some stuff. Which beach do you want to go to?"

Since neither of them was interested in venturing far, they settled for the quiet end of Porthcressa Beach and were soon tucking into a feast of a picnic.

"You never told me what you did that was illegal?" Flynn asked eventually.

Lily frowned. The last few days had been such a blur that it took her a moment to figure out what he was talking about. "Are you asking as a police officer?"

He shook his head and picked up another sausage roll. "Just your boyfriend."

She couldn't control her grin.

"What did you do?" he coaxed.

"Went into Gideon's place through an open window. It was the only place at the retreat I hadn't searched, and Len offered to lend me his ladder so I could get in there."

"That's when he planted the necklace?"

She nodded. "Apparently so. I thought he was helping me search."

"He denied planting it."

"He must have done," Lily said.

"Yeah, I know, but it's also not a bad thing that he's denying it. If he admits it, he might also mention you were with him."

"Oh." She grimaced. "I didn't think about that."

"He hasn't said anything, and I can't imagine he will."

"What's going to happen to him?"

"He has to go to court next week for sentencing. I think he'll spend some time in prison. After that, I guess he'll need to find a new place to live. It would be awkward for him to stay on the islands."

"He completely fooled me," Lily said. "If it weren't for Kit saying he didn't like him, I wouldn't have figured it out."

"What?" Flynn said, and Lily filled him in on that piece of the story and then how smug Kit was now about his character assessment.

She went on to tell him all the other parts of her investigation that she hadn't told him.

"Sorry," she said finally. "I should have told you everything from the start."

"Yeah. You should have."

"I was wondering about the pencil I found at my place, with the name of the art retreat. Do you reckon Len dropped it by accident or on purpose?"

"Who knows? Could have been either, but I imagine he

knew you'd investigate. Leaving you a clue to set you on a wild goose chase makes some sense."

"If he knew I'd investigate, you'd think he might have chosen not to target me."

Flynn began putting lids on the Tupperware boxes. "Apparently, he was holding a grudge against you for getting the lease for the shop. He'd asked about it a while back and been turned down."

"That makes a little more sense then."

With the remaining food cleared away, Flynn patted the space in front of him on the blanket, and she moved to get comfy between his legs, leaning against his chest.

With the sun heading quickly towards the horizon, the sky had turned a vibrant pink with streaks of orange.

"We never talked about what Maria said about your parents," Flynn said.

Her whole body tensed, and a lump swelled in her throat. "I've been avoiding thinking about it."

"You're not tempted to look into it?"

"Very tempted," she said immediately. "Every time I look at my laptop, I think about doing some research and seeing what I can find about the company that wanted to buy my parents' house. I guess I could find that information if I tried."

"But you haven't looked?"

"No. There's been too much going on in my head. I can't deal with it."

"I don't blame you." He fell silent for a few minutes. "We need to talk properly about how we make a long-distance relationship work."

"They don't work," she replied automatically, anger rippling through her.

Flynn didn't argue, just tightened his arms around her. "I love you," he whispered in her ear.

"Don't do that," she snapped, fighting the urge to wriggle out of his embrace.

"What?"

"Tell me you love me just to reassure me."

"That's not why I said it. But if it helps reassure you that we'll be okay, that's a bonus." He threaded his fingers through hers. "When you were growing up, and moving around a lot, did you keep in touch with people?"

She shook her head. "I wasn't allowed. Not when I was a kid anyway, but even when I was a teenager and had more control, it still didn't matter. I had friends, and we swore we'd keep in touch, but it never worked out that way. Out of sight, out of mind, and all that."

"Okay, so it makes sense that you don't think this will work, but I love you. It's never going to be a case of out of sight, out of mind. You've been on my mind pretty much constantly since I met you, and I can't imagine a few hundred miles is going to change that."

She nodded, but didn't believe him.

"I was thinking we could see each other every three weeks."

She turned her head to look questioningly at him.

"I think it'd be realistic for us to visit each other every three weeks. Will you come to London first?"

"In three weeks?"

"Yeah. I want to have a definite date, so when I leave I know when I'll see you again. That would make it easier, wouldn't it?"

"Yeah," she said vaguely. That would make it easier. And three weeks felt manageable. "I could come to London. And it's good if I come before Jessica leaves, so she can open the shop if the weather is decent."

"We'll arrange it so you come on my days off. We can go sight-seeing... or just lie around in bed. Oh, but you also have to meet my mum."

"What?" she said, a small smile pulling at her lips.

"She's desperate to meet you."

"You told her about me?"

"Of course. She's heard all about you."

"I'd like to meet her," Lily mused. "And a few days in London with you sounds like fun."

Her muscles slowly relaxed, and she sank into Flynn's embrace as the sun descended to the horizon. The tips of waves reflected the soft pink light, twinkling gloriously.

"The sunset was worth waiting for," Flynn said, wrapping his arms tighter around her.

"Yes," she turned her face into his neck and inhaled the scent of him.

He'd told her he loved her, and she was very aware that she hadn't said it back. She opened her mouth, but the words wouldn't come.

It felt like a mental block, and it occurred to her it wasn't something she'd said often in her life. Only to her uncle, and definitely not as often as she should have done.

Lifting Flynn's hand to her lips, she kissed his palm.

Hopefully, he knew how she felt about him without her having to say it.

Chapter Forty-Two

THE REST of the week went far too quickly. On Friday evening, Lily and Flynn went to Kit and Seren's place for drinks after his last official day of work. Being with other people was the breath of fresh air they needed, and when the rest of the Trenearys turned up over the course of the evening, along with Ted and PC Hill, it turned into the perfect understated leaving party for Flynn.

It involved a lot of chatter about the new sergeant, who neither Flynn nor PC Hill had taken to. There was also a fun exchange of stories about Sergeant Proctor, which seemed to prepare Lily for the memorial service the following day.

Having that to focus on meant the weekend disappeared with Lily barely having time to think about Flynn's imminent departure. Their plan to see each other helped, though. With that in place, she no longer felt the uncontrolled panic she'd previously had. But she also still hadn't fully rid herself of the notion that he may be able to stay after all.

At least until she was saying goodbye to him in the hallway of her flat. Neither of them was keen on an airport farewell, and since Jago had offered to drive Flynn to the airport, they opted for an unemotional goodbye at Lily's place. It felt like all the other times they'd said goodbye. Just an extended hug and a see you later.

Easy.

Except a little more than an hour after he'd left, she wasn't sure an easy goodbye was what she wanted. She told Jessica she was heading out for a walk and set off toward the airport, gradually increasing her pace while keeping an eye on the sky for the sight of his plane leaving. After being adamant she didn't want an airport goodbye, she was suddenly desperate for one. Especially as there was something she needed to tell him and it suddenly felt imperative.

By the time she had the airport in her sights, she was jogging, and shifted into a sprint as she approached the building.

"Have I missed him?" she called to Jago Treneary when he almost ran her over driving out of the car park.

"I don't know." He grimaced through the open window. "He was about to go through security when I left. Do you want me to wait for you?"

"No, thanks," she said and darted to the entrance. Inside the small building, she didn't have to go far. Relief made her slightly giddy when she spotted Flynn slouched in a chair near the security area with his backpack at his feet. "Aren't you supposed to be getting on a plane?" she called happily.

Flynn's head whipped up, but it was the airport worker nearby who replied.

"He's got about two minutes and then he's missed the plane," he said with a hint of an eye roll.

"What are you doing here?" Flynn asked, standing as Lily approached him.

"Checking you leave. Apparently it's a good job I came." She put her hands on his chest. "What are you doing?"

His shoulders hitched. "Contemplating whether to go. I heard there's going to be a job opening at the ice cream shop soon, so I thought maybe I could work there."

Lily smiled and shook her head. "You'd never make it through the interview process."

"I think I'd be good at scooping ice cream."

"And I think you make a better police officer."

He nodded but didn't look entirely convinced.

"My flight is booked to visit you," Lily said. "I'll see you in three weeks. Everything will be fine."

"When did you get so optimistic?"

"I think one of us should always be optimistic. Apparently it's my turn."

"Will you be okay?" he asked.

"Yes. I promise."

"I'll call you tonight," he said and kissed her until the member of staff cleared his throat loudly.

"You have to go," Lily said.

"It seems like it." He gave her another peck and picked up his backpack.

"Wait," she said, clutching his hand tightly.

"Now you're giving mixed signals."

She shook her head and moved to hug him. "I love you," she murmured against his neck.

"I had a strong suspicion about that." The smile spread quickly across his face. "I love you, too. Now I'm going to leave before one of us starts crying."

With a sigh, she released him. "Go on then."

She watched as he moved through the security area with a backward glance that felt as though it might shatter her heart. Reminding herself she'd see him really soon, she managed a smile, then went to find a window with a view of the tarmac. She didn't move until the plane was in the air.

Sinking into the nearest seat, she let out a sigh. She didn't cry, so that was something. She just needed a minute before she could face going home.

With her head bent, she didn't notice Maria until her hand landed on her shoulder.

"Has he gone?" she asked from the seat beside Lily.

"Yeah." She clasped her hands in her lap. "What are you doing here?"

"Jessica told me you were here." She tilted her head. "I just wanted to check on you."

"I miss him already, but I think I'm okay."

"He seems determined to come back here."

Lily pressed her lips together. "You spoke to him?"

"Yes. I promised him I'd keep an eye on you. I hope that's okay?"

Tears pricked at her eyes then. "It's okay. Thank you."

They fell silent for a few minutes, then Maria spoke again. "There's something I've been wanting to tell you about Derek," she said softly. "It's probably a bad time..."

"Tell me," Lily said.

"I don't even know if this is helpful, or just frustrating, but the last time I spoke to him he'd decided he was going to explain everything to you about your childhood."

Lily inhaled a breath. "He must have changed his mind, because he never mentioned any of it."

"He didn't change his mind, he just didn't have a chance," she said, then paused and took a breath. "The last time I spoke to him was the night before he died."

Lily whipped her gaze to her. "How do you know? I thought you only found out he died when I came to Scilly."

"I already knew." She pushed her hair from her face. "Derek and I hadn't spoken for ages. We only exchanged a few emails over about a decade. He got in touch when the two of you moved back to the UK, but I was married at that time, so we weren't properly in contact. Then he called me out of the blue." She paused and bit down on her lip. "We were on the phone for hours that night. I was divorced by then, and it seemed as though things might finally work out for us. We didn't exactly make any long-term plans, but he was going to come and see me in Bristol the next day and we'd see how things went."

"He didn't turn up?"

"No. I was disappointed, but I thought maybe something had come up and he'd get in touch again. When he didn't answer my calls, I convinced myself that he'd only said he wanted to meet up in the heat of the moment and had changed his mind. I was angry with him – and with myself for letting myself hope things might finally work out. Eventually, I decided I was owed an explanation, and if I had to turn up on his doorstep and demand answers, so be it." She inhaled a dramatic breath. "One of his neighbours told me he'd died. I figured out it must have been right after we spoke."

"I'm sorry," Lily whispered. "Was that when you moved to Scilly?"

"Yes."

"I'd argued with him," Lily said after a moment. "I told him he'd ruined my life by moving me around so much, and that I'd never had a proper home. I was so angry with him."

"He told me all about it."

Lily caught a teardrop at the corner of her eye. "I hate that he died when we were angry with each other."

"He wasn't angry with you." She shook her head. "Not at all. He laughed about your argument. Said it was pretty standard that you'd get in shouting matches, but he thought it got everything out in the open, and he said you'd always apologise to each other later."

"That's true." Lily nodded. "That one felt different though."

"Maybe. He was worried he'd made a mess of your upbringing too. That's why he decided the least he owed you was an explanation. He really was going to tell you everything."

"And I was going to apologise for shouting at him, and for the horrible things I'd said, but he was dead when I got there."

Maria pressed a hand over her mouth. "You found him?"

Lily nodded.

"I'm so sorry," Maria said, her chin trembling madly.

"It's okay," Lily managed, taking Maria's hand.

"And now I'm doubly sorry because I came to check you were okay, and I think you probably were until I arrived."

Lily smiled through tears. "I'm glad you came. I know we're not actually family, but you're the only link I have to my family." She gave a quick shake of her head. "You're not going to leave too, are you?"

"No." She swiped tears from her cheeks. "After Derek died, this felt like where I needed to be. I wasn't sure how long I'd stay, but when I went back to Bristol recently, it was to complete the sale of my house, and pack everything up. I was going to look for my own place here, but Glynis is keen to keep me with her."

Lily grimaced. "Now I feel bad that I have your flat."

"Don't feel bad. It's yours for as long as you want it."

"Thank you." Lily glanced at the door, contemplating getting back to the shop, then she turned back to Maria. "Do you think Uncle Derek was right about what happened with my parents and my gran? That it wasn't an accident."

She looked thoughtful. "I really don't know."

"Did you change your name because of your connection to me and Uncle Derek – did you think you were in danger?"

"I didn't change my name. I just started going by my middle name."

"Because you were scared?"

"Yes. But I really didn't know if Derek was being paranoid or if there was something to his theories."

Lily sat up straighter. "I'm going to find out," she said determinedly.

"What?"

"I'm going to investigate my parents' death."

Maria frowned. "Your uncle couldn't find evidence of anything."

"Because he didn't look properly," Lily said. "He decided that getting me away from the situation was more important than investigating it. I need to get to the bottom of it, once and for all."

Maria bit down on her lower lip. "I don't think Derek would want you poking around in this."

"Well then he should have raised me differently."

He may have brought her up running from problems, but in the end, that was exactly what made her the sort of person who could face anything head on.

Besides, she needed something to keep her from missing Flynn.

Tracking down her parents' killer was exactly the distraction she needed.

To be continued...

Don't miss the next book in the series...

<u>Built on Lies</u>

Some buildings are built on stone... others on secrets.

When amateur sleuth Lily Larkin visits London, she has two things on her mind – spending time with her boyfriend, PC Flynn Grainger, and digging deeper into the mystery of her parents' deaths.

She doesn't expect her trip to involve murder. But trouble has a way of finding Lily... even in the big city.

The residents of Flynn's apartment block are shocked when their landlord, Jeremy Latham, is found dead – crushed beneath his own bookcase. At first, it looks like a tragic accident, until Lily notices inconsistencies among the scattered shelves... and starts hearing unsettling stories about Latham's so-called generosity.

Drawn into a tangle of rivalries, grudges, and whispered complaints, Lily soon realises that everyone had a reason to want Latham gone. But as tensions rise and lies unravel, she must uncover the truth before the killer decides she's asking too many questions.

Because in this building, you can't always trust your neighbours – or your landlord.

Also by Hannah Ellis

The Lily Larkin Series

Death on the Rocks (Book 1)

Malicious Intent (Book 2)

A Poisonous Plot (Book 3)

Dead in the Water (Book 4)

The Sunken Truth (Book 5)

Artful Deceit (Book 6)

The Isles of Scilly Series

The Weekend Getaway (Book 1)

A Change of Heart (Book 2)

The Summer Escape (Book 3)

The Potter's House (Book 4)

An Unexpected Guest (Book 5)

Christmas in the Cotswolds Series

Not Just for Christmas

A Chef's Kiss for Christmas

The Hope Cove Series

The Cottage at Hope Cove (Book 1)

Escape to Oakbrook Farm (Book 2)

Summer at The Old Boathouse (Book 3)

Whispers at the Bluebell Inn (Book 4)

The House on Lavender Lane (Book 5)

The Bookshop of Hopes and Dreams (Book 6)

Winter Wishes in Hope Cove (Book 7)

There's Something about Scarlett (Book 8)

The Single Dads Club Series

It Takes a Village (Book 1)

Riding the Waves (Book 2)

Playing for Keeps (Book 3)

Rules of Engagement (Book 4)

The Loch Lannick Series

Coming Home to the Loch (Book 1)

The Castle by the Loch (Book 2)

Fireworks over the Loch (Book 3)

The Cafe at the Loch (Book 4)

Secrets at the Loch (Book 5)

Surprises at the Loch (Book 6)

Finding Hope at the Loch (Book 7)

Fragile Hearts by the Loch (Book 8)

New Arrivals at the Loch (Book 9)

The Lucy Mitchell Series

Beyond the Lens (Book 1)

Beneath These Stars (Book 2)

Always With You (Standalone novel)

The Friends Like These Series

Friends Like These (Book 1)

Christmas with Friends (Book 2)

My Kind of Perfect (Book 3)

A Friend in Need (Book 4)

Hannah has also written a series of children's books aimed at 5-9 year olds under the pen name, Hannah Sparks. The first book in the *Land of Stars* series is entitled *Where Dragons Fly*.

Printed in Dunstable, United Kingdom

76499090R00138